THE LYON'S SECRET

The Lyon's Den Connected World

Laura Trentham

Dragonblade Publishing, Inc. is an imprint of Kathryn Le Veque Novels, Inc.
P.O. Box 23
Moreno Valley, CA 92556
ceo@dragonbladepublishing.com

Produced in the United States of America

First Edition April 2023
Print Edition

ARE YOU SIGNED UP FOR DRAGONBLADE'S BLOG?

You'll get the latest news and information on exclusive giveaways, exclusive excerpts, coming releases, sales, free books, cover reveals and more.

Check out our complete list of authors, too!

No spam, no junk. That's a promise!

Sign Up Here

www.dragonbladepublishing.com

Dearest Reader;

Thank you for your support of a small press. At Dragonblade Publishing, we strive to bring you the highest quality Historical Romance from some of the best authors in the business. Without your support, there is no 'us', so we sincerely hope you adore these stories and find some new favorite authors along the way.

Happy Reading!

CEO, Dragonblade Publishing

Other Lyon's Den Books

Chapter One

MR. JOSIAH BARRYMORE adjusted his severely-cut black frock coat and pulled the brim of his matching black hat lower over his brow. He was hidden around the corner but with the object of his study in view.

Pots overflowing with spring flowers flanked neat blue doors. The steps were swept and clean, the black iron balustrade devoid of rust. The building was several floors tall and in good repair. Shown just the pretty tableau, he might guess he was in a more fashionable part of town. Not Mayfair, perhaps, but possibly at the townhouse a lesser noble had rented for the season.

But he wasn't anywhere near the fashionable London. He was in Whitehall and staring at the entrance to the Lyon's Den, a popular gaming hell. The two burly former soldiers guarding the door was an irrefutable clue, even if they wore better quality frockcoats than he did.

Subterfuge was a skill he'd perfected during the war, yet he had not been able to ascertain why he'd been summoned to the Lyon's Den. It was disconcerting to realize he was not in possession of the upper hand. He had frequented such places in the past, of course, but his life was different now. If God existed, which he really shouldn't be questioning considering his vocation, he had a sense of humor.

It was afternoon and a steady stream of men entered and exited the gaming hell. Josiah shook his head. The young bucks had too much time and too few brains. Were they supposed to be the cream of English manhood? If so, England was in trouble.

Not for the first time, Josiah wondered how society would shake out if the most intelligent and deserving rose to the top. How many common men would ascend to positions of power? How many women? Instead, England was left with a bunch of namby-pamby wastrels who had gained power by an accident of birth.

Of course, he didn't voice his revolutionary opinions aloud, but while he was not powerful enough to change the tides of a country, he had found ways to cause a ripple. His work wouldn't bring back his friends and comrades who had died, but it helped him sleep at night which was no small thing.

A lull in the foot traffic lured Josiah from around his corner. He strode quickly across the street and took the front steps two at a time. It would not be seemly for him to be spotted entering an establishment that promoted gambling and whoring.

A beefy hand around his lapel held Josiah back from the door. "Whoa, there. Don't recognize you. Are you a member?" The man's Yorkshire accent was broad and thick.

"Prospective," Josiah said.

The second man guarding the door narrowed his eyes at Josiah. He had the lean look of a wolfhound. The type of man whose strength was often underestimated. "Are you one of those zealots come to convert?"

"Not a zealot, but a man of the cloth, yes. Regular old Church of England." Josiah tried on a smile, but neither man was inclined to be charmed.

"Yer not welcome here," the burly man said.

His hand on Josiah's lapel tightened, and Josiah braced for a toss down the stairs, but the wolfhound stopped him with a tap on his forearm. "Wait. The Black Widow surely won't offer a vicar a membership, and if you're not here to convert sinners, then why are you really here?"

The man was unusually astute for someone cast to bounce unruly gentlemen down the steps. Josiah pulled a missive out of the inside pocket of his coat. He had wanted to slip inside and get the lay of the land, but it seemed he was forced to play his trump card. "I was invited by Mrs. Dove-Lyon, your Black Widow."

The lean man took the paper and scanned it. He could read. Josiah hid his surprise. A carriage rattled up and deposited three young gentlemen. They were most likely too young to remember Josiah from his brief stint on society's fringes, but he would rather avoid any potential awkwardness.

"Come on then. I'll take you back," the wolfhound said.

"Thank you," Josiah murmured as they slipped inside the gaming hell before the young men stumbled to the steps.

The smell of tobacco and perfumes mixed in a not-unpleasant way. It brought back a rush of memories Josiah pushed away. He had to keep his wits about him around Mrs. Dove-Lyon.

His guide led him away from the main rooms and down a narrow hallway, opening one of the doors to reveal an empty sitting area. The bright blues and yellows were jarring compared to the minimal, some might say stark, appointments of his cottage next to the church.

"I'll get Mrs. Dove-Lyon." The lean man stepped outside the room, but before he closed the door behind him, he asked, "Where did you serve?"

Josiah huffed a rueful laugh. "All over the Peninsula under Wellington, and then Waterloo, of course. What gave me away?"

"Your eyes. I was at Waterloo as well." The man nodded and left.

Josiah had known that already. Those who had been there were bonded and changed forever even if they'd never met one another before.

The room was airless and windowless. He settled in the large armchair and wondered how long Mrs. Dove-Lyon would let him cool his heels.

Twenty minutes ticked away before the door opened and a woman in black swept inside. She was alone. A black veil covered her face, but as she sank onto the settee across from him, she lifted it.

She was older than the last time their paths had crossed, of course, but still attractive and even more formidable. The business she had built was impressive for anyone, but for a widow to navigate the underworld as deftly as she managed was extraordinary. And worrisome. The terse invitation to attend her was not issued in order to socialize. She wanted something, and it put him on edge.

"Mr. Barrymore."

"Mrs. Dove-Lyon." He dipped his chin.

Her expression didn't change. "May I offer you refreshment?"

"No, thank you. I must return as soon as possible to my flock."

"Ah, yes. Your flock. I was surprised to hear of your current calling. Did you find religion on the battlefield?"

If a god had been at Waterloo, it had been a cruel and vengeful one. "I couldn't remain a solider forever. I needed an occupation."

"But you were never a mere solider, were you, Mr. Barrymore?"

And now she was reaching the point of their meeting. What had she gleaned from her many contacts? "I'm not sure what you mean, Mrs. Dove-Lyon."

She raised an eyebrow and let the silence tighten around them. Many would find themselves babbling to fill the awkwardness, but Josiah was better trained than most. He met her gaze head-on and waited.

Her gaze skipped away from his and he knew a moment of satisfaction, but it evaporated when she said, "A young lady requires assistance."

"What sort of assistance?" he asked warily.

"The sort an unmarried gentleman can provide."

He half-rose from the chair. "Do you mean marriage?"

She waved her hand dismissively. "Goodness, why are you shocked? You can't tell me you are unaware of my activities."

Of course, he made it his business to trace all the threads, no matter how tenuous, that connected people of power. The Black Widow of Whitehall was responsible for a number of high-profile matches amongst the ton. No doubt bribery and blackmail played some part in her success. What leverage did she plan to employ on him?

He settled back into the chair, regretful to have shown even a hint of emotion for her to exploit. "Of course, I am aware, but I am hardly a suitable target. My parish is on the edge of London. I do not circulate in society. The lady I marry must commit to life as a vicar's wife."

"But you do plan to marry." It wasn't a question.

He must marry even if he hadn't the heart for it. Marriage was expected by his parish and by his bishop. The pressure had been increasing over the past months, and the number of young ladies and widows who had happened by his cottage with pies or cakes had become a nuisance, especially when considering the other business he was mixed up in.

"I must eventually marry," he said grudgingly.

"Have you pledged yourself to someone already?"

"Not exactly." He bit the admission out between clenched teeth. "But neither do I require your services in the matter."

"You may very well change your tune when I tell you of the young lady I have in mind." Her tone, too impish for the gravity of the situation, made him think she was taking delight in stringing him along.

He narrowed his eyes. "Am I acquainted with the young lady already?"

"Indeed, you are. She has landed in a spot of bother and came to me as a last resort."

"A spot of bother doesn't require marriage as a solution."

Mrs. Dove-Lyon's gaze sharpened. "Her parents are gone. One brother died in the war; the other has gambled away their fortune. She has a modest inheritance of her own, and her brother is doing his damnedest to get his hands on it. She needs a husband to protect what is hers. Someone strong."

"What is this lady's name?"

"Miss Amelia Fielding."

His breath left him in a long exhale. *Amelia.* She couldn't be of age to marry, could she? The last time he'd seen her, she'd been skinny as a reed and in short skirts. Her brother, Daniel, had been his best friend. They had bought their commissions together, full of bravado and foolishness. And then Daniel had followed Josiah onto a more dangerous path, and Josiah had carried a yoke of guilt since Daniel's death. If-onlys plagued him in the darkest nights.

"Amelia can't be more than . . ." He tried to estimate her age but could only picture her as a young girl.

"She is beyond twenty years of age," Mrs. Dove-Lyon said blandly.

"That's impossible." But of course, it wasn't impossible. Time was a river that carried them all. Over eight years had passed since Josiah and Daniel had marched off to war full of dreams of glory.

From the beginning, Amelia had sent them both letters. It had been a shock to receive the first one, and he'd taken a ribbing from Daniel, but secretly, Josiah had enjoyed the witty nature of the missives. He hadn't written back, of course, not wanting to encourage an infatuation. Yet, letters still arrived every few months.

Things changed after Daniel died. Josiah found himself writing back to Amelia about his grief and guilt. Looking back, it had felt like a confessional. It had certainty been selfish. However, she had offered an absolution that never quite took. Once he'd returned and sold his commission, her letters, if there had been more, were lost to him, and he did not reach out to her with his new direction. He had taken up a new life and assumed she had too.

"Does James owe you money?" he asked. "Are you expecting Amelia to pay?"

Mrs. Dove-Lyon's mouth tightened and her voice was tart. "James has not darkened the door of the Lyon's Den, and if he did, I would have my men toss him out. I knew Amelia's mother, Mrs. Fielding, as a young girl, and I feel a certain sense of responsibility toward her daughter. You may believe it or not, but I can perform a good deed without an ulterior motive, Mr. Barrymore."

Josiah almost apologized, but no doubt, Mrs. Dove-Lyon had been accused of worse. Instead, he worried over the problem of Amelia and solutions that did not entangle him.

Had James gambled away everything? Daniel had spoken about his brother James with equal parts amusement and exasperation. The boy had been spoiled and loved trouble, but Josiah hadn't been aware he'd taken to frequenting gaming hells. The family's estate would have provided a decent income if James had only learned to manage it properly.

Had Daniel lived, he would have made sure James and Amelia were well cared for. Another helping of guilt weighed on Josiah's heart, but surely marriage wasn't his penance. "Daniel spoke of a favored aunt. Can Amelia not seek refuge with her as a companion?"

"Her aunt remarried and is currently sailing to South America, never to return." Mrs. Dove-Lyon paused here to give Josiah a look that might qualify as motherly. "And I will not allow her to work in the Lyon's Den."

"Is that what she wishes to do?" He could not imagine the wide-eyed innocent girl he'd exchanged letters with working in a den of iniquity like the Lyon's Den. Did Amelia understand how the upstairs girls earned their living?

Amusement flashed over Mrs. Dove-Lyon's face. "She does not want to be a burden."

"What happens if I say no?" he asked.

"I don't wish to think on it. Let's discuss instead what would happen if you say yes." Mrs. Dove-Lyon pursed her lips for a moment. "I might be inclined to make a donation to your parish church. I have heard you help returning soldiers when you can."

"I did notice you employ a number of former soldiers."

She inclined her head slightly in acknowledgment. "Don't discount the inheritance Amelia will bring to your marriage. It's not insignificant, and I can't imagine your income is extravagant."

"Neither are my needs." His official income was a pittance, but he had other means that he did not make public. The bishop would strip him of his parish if he was aware of Josiah's secret activities. A wife could prove to be an even greater risk.

Mrs. Dove-Lyon leaned forward. "What is your answer, Mr. Barrymore?"

CHAPTER TWO

A MELIA FIELDING PACED the plush carpet in Mrs. Dove-Lyon's study. It felt like a Covent Garden flower stall had exploded in the small room. Everything that could be upholstered in flowers was. The walls, the chair, the settee, the draperies. It made her nose itch even though the room was bereft of actual flowers.

Her father's study had been full of musty books and excessive masculinity. The scents of tobacco and wet dog had permeated every surface. She had avoided the room as much as possible because it incited sneezing fits, which meant she hadn't seen her father often growing up.

Her mother had been the one to teach her how to read and work her sums. Amelia was fluent in French and Spanish and even knew a little German. She studied conflicts and politics both abroad and closer to home. In between learning how to play the piano forte and drawing, Amelia had also been taught how to shoot and fish.

The family had been comfortable enough to send her brothers to school, but not well-off enough to hire a dedicated governess for her. Any resentment Amelia had harbored at the injustice had been offset by the realization her mother was far more knowledgeable than any governess and allowed her more freedoms.

Losing her father to a fever had been difficult, but losing her mother not a month later had been a blow that still had the power to steal her breath. Her beloved eldest brother, Daniel, had been killed in the war and her aunt was enroute to her new life, which left James, who was useless unless one wanted to end up in the workhouse.

Their mother, of course, hadn't been blind to James's faults and left Amelia the jewelry she had brought into the marriage. Fine, expensive pieces kept in the vault of London's largest bank. Reeking of desperation, James had tried first to cajole Amelia into giving him a ring or necklace to pawn but had moved on to threats when she had stayed firm in her refusal.

Amelia was worse than alone. She was afraid to even pawn the jewelry herself. James and his friends had eyes and ears everywhere. She doubted she would even make it to a pawn broker with the precious stones still in her possession.

Mrs. Dove-Lyon had been a last resort. Amelia's mother had spoken fondly of her childhood friend. They had exchanged occasional letters, but the connection between Amelia and Mrs. Dove-Lyon was tenuous at best. Amelia had no intention of taking advantage of Mrs. Dove-Lyon. She had offered her services wherever needed in the Lyon's Den, but Mrs. Dove-Lyon had forced her to remain veiled or, preferably, to remain out of sight entirely.

A vexing situation to be sure, and one Amelia had circumvented when she could. The upstairs girls enjoyed a good gossip in the kitchens in the early mornings after their patrons had gone, and Amelia had received a different sort of education. One that had left her fanning herself. Her dreams since had been scandalous and only stoked her curiosity.

Had Mrs. Dove-Lyon learned of her fraternization with the staff of the Lyon's Den? Was she going to throw Amelia out on her ear? She had nowhere to go and no one to help her hide from James. Perhaps she could falsify a reference and find a position as a governess or companion. Or she could—

The door to the office opened, and Mrs. Dove-Lyon swept in wearing her customary widow's weeds. Although, Amelia couldn't imagine any other widow wore such finely made mourning dresses. Perhaps the unrelenting black was why Mrs. Dove-Lyon preferred colorful extravagance in her surroundings.

Amelia's pondering stuttered to a halt when she set eyes on the man who trailed Mrs. Dove-Lyon into the room. His sheer masculinity seemed to wilt the flowers around them and made the room seem small and stuffy. She remembered him, of course. How could she forget him when he had made an appearance in so many of her dreams, both by day and night?

The boy she remembered was no longer. Mr. Josiah Barrymore had gained a hardness in and around his eyes and mouth, and laughter seemed a foreign concept to him. He was older and jaded and still just as handsome. Her stomach tumbled and her heart picked up speed in a spate of nervous excitement.

He had accompanied Daniel home for a visit before they had been sent to fight. The two of them had been dressed in their uniforms, clean and starched and unmarred by the reality of war. Mr. Barrymore had been jovial and teased her until she had blushed to the roots of her hair.

It was true she had become enamored of him. She'd sent him a letter on a whim, not expecting him to answer. And he hadn't. Yet, Daniel had mentioned how Josiah seemed to take pleasure in her musings. That was all the encouragement she had needed to continue writing to him. It was only after Daniel's death that she finally heard from him.

The letters they had exchanged had been weighted by a shared grief. A grief she couldn't express to her fragile mother in the months after Daniel's death. His last letter had informed her of his decision to sell his commission now the war was finally over. She hadn't heard from him again, and her subsequent letters had been returned as undeliverable. At the time, it had hurt more than she thought possible. Then, her parents had died, and she learned there were more painful experiences yet.

Was he here to gamble? Or to see one of the upstairs girls? Disappointment filled her at either possibility. "Jos—Mr. Barrymore. This is unexpected."

His gaze seemed to be taking an inventory of her from her braided honey blond hair to her scuffed half-boots peeking out of the hem of her serviceable, high-necked bottle green gown. "You've grown up since last we met." The surprise in his voice took her by surprise.

"It's been years, sir."

"I suppose I have always pictured you as a child."

Of course, he had not returned her childish romantic sentiments, but it stung to hear him imply it nonetheless. "And I still picture you as a young solider full of laughter."

"It seems both our situations have changed."

She shook her head to clear it of the past and turned to Mrs. Dove-Lyon. "This is not a chance meeting with an old friend of my brother's, is it?

"No, indeed. Once I recalled your brother's connection to Mr. Barrymore, I thought of a neat solution to benefit all parties." Mrs. Dove-Lyon took her seat behind the desk and gestured her and Mr. Barrymore toward the chairs.

Amelia sank onto the edge of one chair, too anxious to relax. It was obvious what Mrs. Dove-Lyon intended. Her stomach had turned into a pit of dread. "I do not wish to marry. I already told you I could be an asset to the Lyon's Den. I am—"

"You can't mean to work here, Miss Fielding. Daniel would have never allowed such a thing." Mr. Barrymore was full of indignation.

"Daniel is dead. He can neither help nor judge me." She turned her gaze to Josiah. "And I do not require your judgment either, sir."

"But you could use my help." He looked away and worried a string hanging from his cuff. "It so happens a good marriage might favor my circumstances as well."

What were his circumstances? Why would an eligible young gentleman need to marry in haste? Was he no better than James and his ilk, manipulating her into signing over her inheritance?

She studied him closer now. He was dressed all in black, except for a white shirt and simply knotted stock of white linen around his neck. While well-made and of quality cloth, his clothes were severe and absent any adornment. He had never been a popinjay, but she could recall how his red regimental uniform had brought out the color in his cheeks and made his dark eyes sparkle.

"Why are you dressed so soberly?" she asked, suddenly suspicious.

"I'm dressed as befits my calling."

"You're a *vicar*?" Never had he given any indication in his letters that he was called to a higher power. Not a single quote from the Bible. Not even a blessing. It was preposterous to picture him giving a sermon, and just as preposterous to think she would be his helpmate. She popped to her feet and swung toward Mrs. Dove-Lyon. "Do you honestly think I would make a suitable wife for a vicar?"

"For the average vicar, no. But, for Mr. Barrymore? Perhaps." Mrs. Dove-Lyon remained impassive in the face of Amelia's shock and dismay.

Amelia swung around to glare at Josiah. "Doesn't the Bible say 'Blessed are the meek?'"

"Yes."

"I'm not meek. I would make a terrible wife for you."

The corners of his mouth lifted in what might have been the start of a smile but it was gone before Amelia could decide. "Believe me, Miss Fielding, I did not come here seeking a wife."

"Yet, here you are." Amelia set her hands on her hips. "You haven't run away screaming in horror, so I can only surmise you are considering Mrs. Dove-Lyon's mad scheme."

"It's not mad. It's practical."

Amelia rolled her eyes heavenward and injected as much dripping sarcasm as she could into her voice. "Please, stop. I'm near to swooning from your romantic declarations."

And if the morning hadn't been full enough of shocks, Josiah laughed.

It was a lovely laugh. Husky and deep and the first true thing she recognized of the man she used to know. It made the old sparkle leap back into his eyes, and his smile revealed his straight white teeth. She remembered now why she had become infatuated with him as a young girl. As a woman, however, she felt a different sort of tug toward him. It was a yearning deep in her belly.

Oh dear. Perhaps a month ago, she would have had no idea what the feeling was, but she had listened to the upstairs girls enough to know exactly what the empty longing signified. She desired him. Or at least her body desired his. This sort of feeling did not involve the head or the heart. It was entirely animal in nature.

She regained her seat and folded her hands primly on her lap. "You cannot force me to marry. Neither of you can. I will simply walk to the bank and take one of my mother's necklaces to a shop to sell. Then, I shall . . ." What on earth would she do? James would never leave her alone.

"We have been over this. James is desperate." Mrs. Dove-Lyon's exasperation was palpable. "I doubt you'd make it out of the bank before he nabbed you and forced an elopement with one of his cronies."

"Can you give us a moment in private, Mrs. Dove-Lyon?" Josiah framed it as a question, but the authority in his voice did not invite dissent.

Even so, Amelia was surprised Mrs. Dove-Lyon ceded the room

without a protest. It was beyond the pale to leave an unmarried young lady alone with a gentleman, even a vicar. Then again, neither unmarried young ladies nor vicars usually frequented gaming hells.

Once they were alone, Josiah rose and paced to the window. He stood to the side of the sash and peeked out. It struck her as an odd mannerism, but she had other more pressing issues to consider.

"I can't believe you are even entertaining the idea of this marriage, Mr. Barrymore."

He turned from the window and resumed his pacing. "I remember when you called me Josiah."

"That was a long time ago." A festering hurt welled up. "Two years, in fact! You stopped writing. My father then my mother died. I thought I might hear from you then."

Blast the tears that sprang into her eyes. She turned away from him to pretend to study the shelves behind the desk.

"I am sorry, Amelia. More than you can know. Once I returned, I needed to leave the past behind and decided it was best for both of us not to cling to Daniel's ghost any longer."

She could sense him moving closer to her. "You assumed what was best for me. You were the only one I could be honest with. I needed you."

"I didn't know about your parents' passing until much later. I should have come to pay my respects. Can you forgive me?"

Even as she accused him of abandoning her, she knew it was unfair of her. He was not responsible for her in any way. Not then, and not now.

"I am no longer a child. I do not need rescuing." She turned to face him, finding him closer than she expected. The fractured blues and greens of his eyes drew her in.

"No, you are most definitely a woman grown." His gaze skimmed down her body and his husky voice held an insinuation that made her stomach clench. Softly, he added, "Asking for help does not mean you are weak, Amelia."

She could insist he call her Miss Fielding, yet she found herself replying in a tart tone, "You don't wish to wed me. Admit it."

He rubbed his chin which was shadowed with whiskers. Weren't vicars required to shave every morning? "The pressure for me to marry has been intensifying. My flock and my bishop wish it."

Amelia wasn't dumb or blind. She knew exactly how the unmarried women in his flock would react to a clergyman who looked like Josiah. "It's only fair that you pick one of the ladies from your flock. I'm sure they're lined up out the door for you."

"What are you implying?"

"Oh, please." Amelia rolled her eyes in a very unladylike manner and returned his stare. "Do your vows preclude ownership of a looking glass? You are a handsome, eligible gentleman with an income. You have good teeth, good hair, and I expect are pox free. You are a catch."

"What in the—" Knowing she was the cause of the look of consternation and shock on his face was exhilarating. He shook his head. "I assume you haven't kept to your room as Mrs. Dove-Lyon instructed."

"I assume you remember a few moments ago when I told you I wasn't meek. It was not bluster." She raised her brows.

"Believe it or not, meek women do not attract me." His shock had morphed into a look of contemplation that she did not like.

"I'm sorry Mrs. Dove-Lyon wasted your time. As you can see, I am well. I merely need to plan my next move. I don't need your help," she repeated with emphasis.

"You are lying to me and, perhaps, even to yourself. You do need help. It's why you came to Mrs. Dove-Lyon in the first place. She cannot help you, but I can. How short is James on coin?"

How had he seen through her bravado so easily? The fear she'd kept at bay bubbled up. "He has vowels all over town and hasn't a feather to fly with from what I have gathered. Bond Street has stopped extending him credit. His reputation is tattered."

"Your inheritance would come under the purview of your husband. Has James tried to marry you to one of his degenerate friends?"

She nodded, unable to put her helpless anger into words. It was worse than that, of course, because she wouldn't marry willingly. James's plan involved her ruination. It was her turn to gaze out the window. "I can't believe he could sink so low. I'm his sister."

"Men are capable of great cruelty." His experience added gravitas to the sentiment.

Through Daniel's letters, and later Josiah's, she understood better than most what horrors they had faced.

Was marrying Josiah such a terrible choice? For the young girl who still lived inside of her, it would be her dreams come true, but dreams could turn into nightmares. "If we marry, will you confiscate my inheritance and pocket the proceeds?"

"Your inheritance would belong to you. I promise not to touch it. You can do with it what you will."

She turned and searched his face to gauge his honesty. Yes, he was a vicar, but there were dishonest people in every walk of life. He met her gaze straight-on and didn't retreat.

"Do you swear to God?" she asked.

"I do." His lips twitched again before settling into a firm line. "You would have a great amount of freedom if we marry. There is no high society to please in Upper Wexham."

"Surely there are duties you will expect me to perform."

"Attending Sunday services." He shrugged. "The rest will be up to you."

"I can laze about in bed all day?" A scoffing sound got caught in her throat when he leaned forward, leaving their faces close.

Feeling every bit of her inexperience, she retreated until her heels hit the wall next to the window. He followed her, bracing his hands on either side of her shoulders. Heat flared between them. Enough to bring a telling blush to her face.

She was effectively trapped, yet felt no panic. Instead, her fingers twitched with the urge to run up his chest and inside his jacket. She tucked her hands between the wall and the small of her back.

"Only if you occasionally allow me to join you."

Her blood turned to honey at the unmistakable dark promises in his words. The thick, sweet pulse made her knees tremble. "Our marriage would be a real one, then?"

His gaze dropped to her mouth which went suddenly dry. She darted her tongue over her bottom lip, and she caught his swift intake of breath.

"I'm a vicar, not a monk, and you are a beautiful woman." All playfulness evaporated, and his brow furrowed. "But only if a real marriage is what you want."

The warmth from his words made her heart sing. "And if I said I wanted a marriage in name only?"

"Is that what you want? Can you not imagine ever sharing my bed?" His mouth softened, and his eyes became hooded. Her body reacted in kind, her head tipping back slightly.

Goodness, now it was all she could imagine, even though she was short on the actual details of what sharing his bed would entail. Tangled sheets and bare skin were foremost in her mind.

"I'm not sure what I want." That was a lie. And a terrible sin considering she was lying to a man of the cloth. But she could hardly admit she wanted to know what his body felt like against hers.

His voice dropped in timbre. "Let's not play games about something so serious. Your curiosity is obvious. Are you still a virgin?"

The question shocked her coming from a vicar but also because he asked with no hint of impending hell and damnation at her answer. "Does it matter?"

"It matters in how gentle I should be the first time."

"Oh. Very practical. In that case, yes, I am still a virgin." She cleared her throat, trying for a teasing tone but landing closer to breathless shock. "Will you be rough with me after the first time?"

His gaze popped back to hers, his eyes flaring. "Only if you wish it."

Amelia's mind whirred over conversations she had been privy to over the past week. Comments and giggles she did not fully understand at the time were suddenly illuminated. It wasn't disgust she was feeling but a dangerous level of titillation. "Do you wish it?"

CHAPTER THREE

THE IMAGE OF pounding into Amelia from behind with his hand wrapped in her hair popped into his head. Did he wish to take her roughly? Unequivocally, yes. In fact, he wished to take her many times over in every way possible. Rough, gentle, teasing, serious.

Amelia blinked up at him with innocent eyes. Well, perhaps she wasn't as innocent as she appeared with her rosy cheeks, wide dark blue eyes, and honey blond hair considering the direction of their conversation.

Before he'd stepped into the room to meet her again after so long, he'd decided he must do the honorable thing for his friend and marry her. If Daniel were alive, Amelia would be safe in the country doing whatever she enjoyed. Milking cows perhaps?

She certainly had the look of a toothsome milkmaid. Wholesome yet with an underlying sensuousness that took him by surprise. Gone was the skinny young girl and in her place was a woman with a full bosom and curves that would tempt any man. Even a vicar.

Especially this vicar. Josiah shifted his hips to relieve the growing consequence of his abstinence. He had not been with a woman for too long. Not because he had bought into the strict morality of the church but because he knew better than to dally with any of the women in Upper Wexham who maneuvered for a deeper connection. Namely marriage. Yet, here he was committing to a young lady out of a sense of obligation.

The closer he stood to her the less a marriage felt like an obligation. Based on his reaction to her and the curiosity he could sense in her, he hoped she would realize the benefits of their union.

"I can only imagine the tales the young women have shared in this establishment." He decided it best to evade her question.

"Absolutely toe-curling. Some of the girls enjoy servicing the men, but some don't." Her gaze was direct, and he appreciated not having to deal with fluttering eyelashes and coy glances.

"Every job becomes tiresome."

"Won't it be my duty to . . ." She bit her bottom lip.

"Service me?" He found his lips curling into a smile. It had happened more than once in her company already. Of course, he smiled until his cheeks hurt at his parishioners on a Sunday, but the smiles she was coaxing out of him were spontaneous and warmed him in ways he couldn't describe.

"Does this mean you are willing to share my bed as a true wife?" He tensed, her answer more important than he could fathom, considering he had followed Mrs. Dove-Lyon into the room as if the gallows awaited.

"Yes," her whisper sent a shiver through him. "But what if we don't suit? What if I'm like the girls who do not enjoy the act?"

He moved his hands from the wall to her shoulders and pulled her closer. Her body was soft, and she smelled sweet and innocent. His nose brushed against hers, and her sharp intake of breath swelled his chest with satisfaction. She leaned into him, her curves cradling him and firing an unexpectedly intense desire.

"We will both find pleasure in our marriage bed," he murmured.

"How can you be sure?" Her voice had taken on a husky quality he found appealing.

"Because of the way your body is reacting to mine, and mine to yours."

Her face turned to his like a sunflower seeking the sun, and he dropped his mouth to hers in a gentle kiss. This would be an introduction to the pleasures they could share. He deepened the kiss, slowly and with enviable control, considering how he longed to ravage her mouth.

But the last thing he wanted was to scare her. He did not relish a fearful woman in bed. He would have waited if she had insisted, but the relief of her agreement to consummate the marriage had made his knees wobble. He'd never been so instantly attracted to a woman on first sight. Of course, she wasn't entirely a stranger. He knew her to be intelligent, funny, and adventurous from her letters. It seemed she had retained the traits even into womanhood.

Her hands were on the move. She gripped the sides of his waistcoat and pulled their hips closer, and then she skimmed her fingers beneath his coat to clutch his shoulders. When he tried to cant his hips away, she slipped a leg around his calf and didn't allow him to shield her from his desire.

Unable to stop himself, he pushed her against the wall and pressed his erection into the softness of her belly. He caught her wrists and held her hands over her head so he could fully feel the length of her body against his. He cursed the layers of clothes keeping her soft breasts and peaked nipples from his mouth.

"Is this what you want, angel?" He ground his hips against her. If he wasn't careful, he might spend in his trousers like a schoolboy in the middle of a dream.

"I don't know. I feel strange."

"Tell me."

"Uncomfortable. Intense. I thought it would be different. Less . . . frustrating."

"Do you want me to stop?" It would take the strength of Hercules to step away, but somehow he would manage it.

"No. Stopping will make it worse. I need *more*." She nipped his bottom lip.

He kissed her without holding back this time. His tongue twined with hers, and she squirmed against him. He transferred her wrists to one hand and trailed the other to her breast, squeezing gently. She lifted her mouth away with a gasp, her pupils dilated and her cheeks pink.

"I know what you need and will happily give it to you. Anytime and anywhere you wish once we're married." He spoke against her neck and then took a light bite of the tender skin.

"Are you really a vicar?" Her voice was reedy.

A laugh rumbled out of him. "Not the best or most pious vicar, but yes." The understatement made him smile even wider.

Her lips were full and reddened from their kisses, and when she bit her bottom lip to stem an answering smile, he nearly swooped for another. If he didn't stop himself now, he would have her skirts up and his trousers down before good sense could insert itself.

He let go of her wrists and tried to step away, but she held him by the shoulders. If he were being perfectly honest, he didn't want to let her go. It was a wholly disconcerting experience. He forced himself to step away from her, out of arm's reach.

She leaned against the wall, looking bemused and frustrated and very thoroughly aroused. "When will we marry?"

As if on cue, a knock sounded and the door opened. Mrs. Dove-Lyon swept inside. She glanced between them. "A decision has been reached."

It was not a question, and Josiah did not attempt to make excuses for their behavior. Lord knows, the woman had seen worse. "We will marry. We were just discussing the timing and particulars. Reading the banns will take—"

"No. There is no time for such conventions even if you are of the clergy." Mrs. Dove-Lyon sat behind her desk. "A special license is in order."

"I doubt it would be issued to me, and the cost is too dear." He had the coin, but preferred to use it elsewhere.

"I called in a favor from a gentleman patron, and the license is on its way. All you need do is sign." The satisfaction in her voice was like sandpaper.

"You were confident I would be so malleable to your plans?" Josiah was more admiring than offended at her high-handedness.

"Unfortunately for you, it's your nature to act honorably."

He wanted to argue the point by listing all the dishonorable tasks he had performed, but she wasn't wrong. Those missions had cost him—they were like cuts to his soul that would never heal.

Amelia stepped into the fray with her hands on her hips and a mulish expression. "You assumed I would agree to marry a man I hadn't laid eyes on in years?"

"Of course, my dear." Mrs. Dove-Lyon's voice had softened slightly, but still held an edge. "For one thing, you have few other choices that do not involve your ruination. Secondly, you were infatuated with Mr. Barrymore as a young girl. I knew you would not turn down an offer to marry him."

"How did you—I was not—" Amelia crossed her arms over her chest. "That is ridiculous."

With fascination, Josiah watched pink creep up her neck into her cheeks. She was flustered and it was . . . charming. With difficulty, he turned his attention back to Mrs. Dove-Lyon. "And this effort is completely altruistic on your part?"

"Well, as to that . . ." Mrs. Dove-Lyon steepled her hands and tapped her chin. Her calculating look sent a chill through him. "I would ask a boon in return."

"What boon?" His dread was growing by the second.

Mrs. Dove-Lyon made an expansive gesture with her hands. "I don't know yet, but I'm sure your . . . talents will prove useful."

The Black Widow of Whitehall had survived and thrived for a reason. It was obvious she was aware he led a life outside of the vicarage. Being indebted to her did not settle well, but it turned out she had discovered the leverage she needed. He wanted Amelia through whatever means necessary, and she would be in his bed tonight if he agreed. The temptation was too strong to override his logic.

"Fine," he bit out.

"Very good." Her smile made him feel as though he'd been truly caught in a black widow's web. Mrs. Dove-Lyon's smile softened when she turned it on Amelia. "Go pack your things and say your good-byes. Several of the girls are in the kitchens."

Amelia nodded and slipped out the door. The silence she left behind was filled with portents. He refused to be the one to break it.

Finally, Mrs. Dove-Lyon said, "You can't be terribly upset at our deal. You obviously find the chit agreeable."

"As any man would. She is lovely."

"And headstrong and intelligent. Most men do not appreciate those particular qualities in a woman. Her dissolute brother certainly doesn't."

"James is a fool."

"Which only makes him more dangerous and unpredictable. You will be able to protect her." While it wasn't a question, Mrs. Dove-Lyon paused, clearly expecting a response.

"Do you expect James to kick up trouble even after we are married?"

"He will not be happy."

"I will keep Amelia safe. It's the least I can do for Daniel. What about you?"

"What about me?" She raised a brow in a way that made him feel foolish, yet he carried on.

"If James discovers you helped Amelia, he could turn his anger on you."

She gestured expansively. "I am well protected by my boys."

Based on the two former soldiers at the front door, Josiah decided not to waste his worry on Mrs. Dove-Lyon and her Den.

Amelia returned wearing a fetching bonnet of cream with forest green ribbons and set a traveling bag inside the door. The license arrived, and he decided not to question the blackmail it had required to obtain. The marriage took place with little emotion and no fanfare.

And then it was time to start their life together as man and wife.

He picked up the bag and shot Amelia a look of surprise. "Did you bring bricks from your family home?"

"Don't be silly. I brought some favorite books. I fully expect James to gamble away the house and all its contents. I wanted a few mementos." She tightened the ribbons of her bonnet and adjusted her gloves.

How must Amelia be feeling? He was overwhelmed and more than a little in shock at the turn the day had taken. He certainly hadn't woken with the thought that he would be going to bed that evening a married man, but at least he would be doing it in familiar surroundings. The vicarage was comfortable, but hardly as big and grand as the house Amelia grew up in.

She'd run away from her home to escape a brother who had no love for her and landed in a gaming hell. She had just been married off to a man she barely knew. He was taking her to a house she had never seen in a village where she knew no one. And tonight, she would share his bed which he had heard could be a traumatic, emotional experience the first time for a woman.

Yet, she was not maudlin and showed no fear. She seemed the type of person who would make the best of any situation. It was admirable.

He offered her the crook of his arm. "Are you ready?"

"I am." She blew out a sharp breath and graced him with a smile although it was small and tight.

They left from a side door to avoid being seen. Eventually James would find out about their marriage, but there was no reason to hasten that day.

He flagged down a hack to take them to the inn where he'd left his small curricle and horse stabled. On the brief journey, they made unimportant conversation about the weather in between silences.

The inn was on a well-travelled road out of London. He often stopped in or used it as a meeting place because there were no regular patrons to remember him. Travelers passed through on their way to somewhere else which meant he could come and go with few questions.

The owner, Haney, was a man well into his middle age who had lost a son in the war, and he was an excellent source of information based on his position. Information he was well-paid for. It was an exchange that suited them both.

Although Haney looked curious as to why he was returning with a young woman in tow, he did not question Josiah, only nodded and offered some innocuous tidbits of gossip gleaned from travelers. Even though none of the information seemed worth much, Josiah passed along a few coins. More than enough to cover his brief use of the inn's stable.

Josiah and Amelia were finally alone on the road, the brisk breeze ruffling her skirts. They were sitting close enough that their thighs were pressed against one another. After a quarter hour of brisk travel, Josiah slowed and steered them from the wide main road onto a narrower lane toward Upper Wexham. The wheels bumped over ruts and into holes jostling Amelia into him.

"I apologize for the tight quarters. I wasn't expecting to bring home a . . . wife." He choked slightly on the word.

"It's difficult to fathom, isn't it?" Her small laugh was humorless.

"I'm not sure how to feel about our situation."

Josiah glanced over, but her bonnet shielded her expression. "Mrs. Dove-Lyon intimated you might have viewed me with some fascination when you were young, and I assumed as much based on your early letters."

"It is true that you cut quite a figure in your regimentals when you came home with Daniel. Of course, that was before I knew anything of the world." She was speaking briskly, her words almost tripping over one another in her haste to give an excuse.

Yet, somewhere in his chest, a coal he thought blackened and cold, flared with warmth. In a teasing voice, he asked, "And now that you are more worldly, what do you think of the severe black uniform of my profession?"

She squirmed and Josiah opened his mouth to put her out of her misery, but she said, "You are appealing in whatever you wear. I can only imagine what you thought of me so many years ago."

"I thought you were sweet and entertaining."

"Like a puppy." This time her laugh was rueful but genuine.

He sent a longer look in her direction. Her eyes remained hidden by the brim of her bonnet, but he could see her smile. "You were still a child then. You grew up to be a beautiful woman, Amelia. It has left me feeling unbalanced."

"That is very kind of you to say." Her voice was smaller now, and he felt the need to drive his point home.

He transferred the reins into one hand and covered her gloved hands with his own. "It is true. You are lovely, and my hope is that we will rub along well together."

She whipped her head around to look him in the eyes. "Rub along well? Don't you wish for something greater? I don't expect love, of course, but can we not hope for some measure of happiness, perhaps?"

He swallowed past an unexpected slug of emotion and spoke a truth he had tried to hide away from everyone, even himself. "I don't remember how to be happy."

He could feel her gaze on his face as if trying to decipher him. What did she see? A man who was a shell of the young solider she had admired so many years ago? A man living a lie and taking risks to pay his penance?

His well-trained horse didn't need guidance, but he turned his attention back to the road to avoid Amelia's probing stare. He was walking along a cliff's edge. She must be kept in the dark about his non-clergy-related duties. After all, he had promised Mrs. Dove-Lyon to keep her safe.

They had left the buildings of London behind and fields being plowed by draft horses took their place. Upper Wexham was still a bucolic village full of farmers and tradesmen, but Josiah could envision a future where it was overtaken by an ever-expanding London.

He pointed ahead. "And here we are. Your new home."

CHAPTER FOUR

AMELIA SAT FORWARD on the carriage seat. The spire of a white clapboard church reached upward through the trees. The cottages popping up beside the road were well maintained and many were of an older style with thatching.

"It's very picturesque," she said.

A woman working to prune a large rose bush with a pair of pruning shears sent them a wave and curious glance, but Josiah only nodded and continued on. "Widow Hamilton is a good woman but one of the biggest gossips in town. She has two daughters. We can expect a visit tomorrow on some pretext or other."

Amelia bit her lip and smoothed her dress. The reality of serving as a vicar's wife was beginning to set in. Her unconventional education and the lack of social polish left her feeling uncertain. Would the ladies of Upper Wexham accept her?

As if sensing her inner turmoil, Josiah said, "There's no need to be nervous. On the whole, the town is friendly and the people welcoming."

"Will there be jealousy you wed an outsider and not one of the young women of your congregation?" she asked.

His hesitation was answer enough, but the slight questioning lilt in his voice grew the pit in her stomach. "I don't think so?"

"Oh dear. Would it be unseemly if I actually did hide under the covers for the next few weeks?" She was only half-joking. Another thought occurred to her. She shifted and grabbed his sleeve. "I don't know how to cook, Josiah. A woman from the village came to our house for the cooking. We are going to starve."

He graced her with the twinkling of a half-smile, his gaze still on the road ahead which was growing busier with people walking or riding. "I employ a housekeeper who also cooks my meals. That doesn't need to change."

Relief did little to settle her nerves. Fleeing her home into the unknown had meant being dogged by a constant anxiety. Yes, she had outwitted James, but had she only replaced one dilemma with another by marrying Josiah?

What sort of husband would Josiah make? It would have been best to consider the question before she had signed her future into his hands. She stared at his profile. His nose was a blade, and his chin jutted stubbornly. His hazel eyes were framed by a strong brow and broad cheeks. His hair looked blondish in the sun but darkened to a light brown in the shadows. He wasn't handsome in any sort of classical sense, but he was undeniably attractive.

More important than his looks was his temperament. He was serious, but she had seen flashes of humor. Would he be kind or cruel or simply indifferent toward her? Her father had been the indifferent sort, leaving her mother to do as she willed. Did Amelia wish the same?

He handled the reins with his bare hands. They were strong and tanned. Not the hands of a man who spent his days studying holy texts and writing sermons. She imagined him touching her with those hands. What would it feel like? She supposed she would find out soon enough. A pleasant squirmy feeling took hold in her belly.

They turned onto a narrow lane lined with pretty greenery. The white clapboard church greeted them at the end. And tucked to the side, with the stones of a cemetery rising in between, was a two-story house, larger than she expected, but unadorned and simple. Behind the church and house was a copse and beyond that a field she could barely make out through the trees. Even though they were close to the village, it felt secluded—except for the dead—and a shiver went down her spine.

A small stable of weatherworn planks stood to the side of the house, only big enough for two or three horses and the carriage. No groom ran out to greet them. Josiah climbed down and came around to offer his help. She found herself being lifted down, his hands firm around her waist. He didn't immediately release her, his body pressed close enough to feel the heat. She looked up at him, feeling flustered, intending to make a joke, but her tongue tangled and nothing came out.

His stare was intense and burning. "I realize marrying a vicar with little to his name was not the dream you held of your future. I will do my best to make sure you don't regret your decision, Amelia."

Sudden tears pricked. It was true, of course. Her dreams had consisted of a marrying a gentleman with an extensive library and the freedom of doing whatever she pleased with her time. There would be expectations as Josiah's wife. Expectations she wasn't sure she could satisfy.

"Women have little choice in our futures. I must accept my lot." The words were out before she could take them back. His only reaction was the slight narrowing of his eyes, but for some reason, she got the impression she had hurt his feelings, even if what she said was true. Hastily, she added, "I hope we can find a measure of happiness together."

"As do I." He released her, and she missed the feel of his hands squeezing her waist. "I am kept quite busy, and you will have a good amount of freedom to pursue your own interests. As I said before, I would only ask you plan to attend Sunday services."

"Of course," she said.

He hauled down her bag and stepped into the house. She followed, and looked around, taking a deep breath. The scent was fresh and clean with a hint of cooking food. The entrance was modest and absent any decoration. There were no pictures on the walls or flowers or even a table to set them on. It wasn't warm or welcoming, but she could see the promise of both. One or two pictures and a vase of flowers would brighten the space.

A hall led to the back of the house where she assumed the kitchen was located. A comfortable sitting room was to their right. She could picture Josiah seated in front of the fire sipping brandy and reading. She would need to find a second chair for herself, or perhaps she would prefer the settee. It looked comfortable enough. Would he expect her to darn his socks?

Footsteps swung her attention around. A woman of middle years with steel-gray hair pulled back into a severe bun marched down the hall, wiping her hands on a worn apron with a few old and new stains to mar the white. This must be the housekeeper and someone Amelia needed to win over. She slapped a smile on her face.

"Mr. Barrymore, you've returned. I received word that—" The woman broke off when she caught sight of Amelia. The woman shot Josiah a sharp look. "I wasn't expecting you to return with company, sir."

"Not just company, Mrs. Drinkwater. This lady is my wife, Mrs. Amelia Barrymore." A firm hand on Amelia's lower back drew her forward.

"How do you do, Mrs. Drinkwater?" Amelia offered her hand, but thought better of her action when Mrs. Drinkwater merely stared at it in shock. Just as the moment veered into awkwardness, Mrs. Drinkwater gave Amelia's fingers a slight squeeze of acknowledgment.

"A wife? This wasn't part of the plan." Mrs. Drinkwater's tone held a familiarity but also a warning.

It occurred to Amelia the woman must be worried about losing her position in the household. "I realize I am a disruption, but I hope you will continue in your current capacity. Sadly, I am not well-versed in the household duties of a wife."

Josiah drew her closer into his side as if offering her protection. "Amelia is Daniel Fielding's sister. She found herself in dire straits."

"And marriage was the only option?" Mrs. Drinkwater's voice was terse.

"It was." Josiah held Mrs. Drinkwater's gaze until she rolled her eyes as if giving in.

The housekeeper turned her attention to Amelia, her expression softening slightly. "I did not know your brother personally, but I have heard he was a good man and a favorite amongst his fellow soldiers."

"That is very kind of you. He is greatly missed." The grief had faded over the past months, and Amelia found a smile at the memories of her brother.

"Allow me to show you the rooms upstairs while Mr. Barrymore sees to the carriage." Mrs. Drinkwater shot another sharp glance in Josiah's direction that was disapproving in a motherly way. "Only one chamber has been appointed properly."

Once upstairs, they passed by a small room that appeared best outfitted for a monk. It contained a pallet on the floor and a single stand with a washbasin. Her questions got tied on her tongue when they entered the larger of the upstairs rooms. In contrast, a large bed dominated this room. Dark blue velvet hangings were tied back to the four posters to reveal a thick mattress piled high with covers. It was decadent. A blush spread through Amelia as she gaped.

"Mr. Barrymore had the bed brought in especially. It took four men to winch the down mattress through yonder window. He said that he spent too many nights on the cold hard ground and refused to sleep on the cot the former vicar used."

"I'm thankful not to be spending my wedding night on a cot," Amelia said when she finally found her tongue.

"No doubt you would like to freshen up. I'll bring up a basin of warm water for you." Mrs. Drinkwater was at the door.

"That's not—" The door shut on Amelia's protest. She didn't want the housekeeper to think she needed to be waited on. Surely, Amelia could figure out how to heat water. But her confidence wasn't great enough to follow Mrs. Drinkwater down the stairs.

She perched on the edge of the bed for a moment. If she was going to freshen up, she would need her things. Feeling like an interloper, she tiptoed down the stairs. Her traveling bag was sitting by the door. Voices stopped her with her hand on the handles.

Curiosity was a blessing and a curse and maybe a sin if it led her to eavesdrop. Yet, she couldn't help herself. She crept past the sitting room and halfway down the hall toward the kitchen, keeping in the shadows.

"—our endeavors. A wife? Are you mad?" It was Mrs. Drinkwater, and she sounded exasperated.

"James, her brother, is a bounder who is deeply in debt and desperate for her inheritance."

"Inheritance? And now it is ours." The satisfaction in her voice set the hairs on the back of Amelia's neck to quivering.

"No. I promised her I wouldn't touch her inheritance."

"How many promises have you made and broken?" she asked harshly.

"Never with intention. I don't plan to break my promise to Amelia."

Mrs. Drinkwater made a sound of disappointment. "Why on earth would you marry the chit then? She could upend the entire operation if she proves to have a loose tongue."

What on earth had Amelia stumbled into? The relationship between Mrs. Drinkwater and Josiah clearly went beyond vicar and housekeeper.

"I owe it to Daniel to protect his sister." Josiah sounded defensive and not like the housekeeper's employer.

"And she is quite comely. Are you saying that had nothing to do with your rash decision?"

"I'll not deny an attraction. I might be a vicar, but I'm still a man." His admission inspired warmth in her chest.

Her mother had been more concerned with her mind than her outward appearance, and her father had treated her as an afterthought. He had two sons to occupy his ambitions. A girl was little use to him beyond the possibility of an advantageous marriage. No one had ever called her comely or lovely or any of the things Josiah made her feel.

"At least you acknowledge the truth." Mrs. Drinkwater gave a huffing laugh at this, and some of the tension between them seemed to dissipate. "I promised the girl warm water."

"I'll take it."

Amelia scurried to grab her bag and get back up the stairs before she was caught eavesdropping. The squeak of the next to last step made her cringe but she didn't look over her shoulder.

She set her bag at the end of the bed and began unpacking, cocking her ear to listen for the creaking step. She stacked her books on a side table by the bed and was pulling out her gowns when Josiah entered. She had not heard his approach on the stairs.

He set a basin full of steaming water on a hip-high wash stand and turned toward her, rubbing his hands together. Their wedding night was fast approaching, and Amelia couldn't stop herself from glancing toward the bed in the room. He did the same. Awkwardness descended.

He turned away first. "You can hang your dresses in the wardrobe and . . ." He opened the top drawer of the chest and scooped out the clothes there, piling them into a different drawer. "You can have the use of this drawer for your underthings." He cleared his throat.

She hung the dresses in the wardrobe and gathered her stockings and garters and chemises into her arms to tuck away in the chest. Her meager belongings barely covered the bottom. She allowed herself to dwell on what she had left behind for only as long as it took to close the drawer. Her future was standing before her. She tried to smile, but found her lips uncooperative.

"I would like to wash and change, and then . . ." What happened next? She was in uncharted waters.

"Mrs. Drinkwater has a hearty stew made, and there is fresh bread from the baker. I'm afraid the dining room table has become a repository for the flotsam of my life. I'll clean it all away this week. I usually eat in the kitchen, but if you'd prefer, we can—"

"I don't wish to disrupt your life. The kitchen is fine."

He took her by the shoulders. "My life will now widen to include you. It's a disruption, but not an unwelcome one. I was fast becoming a monk instead of a vicar. It will take time though, I think, for us to learn one another's idiosyncrasies."

That was the truth. Already she had questions about his housekeeper and what operation Amelia might upend. If Mrs. Drinkwater wasn't matronly enough to be his mother, she might suspect an affair, but their relationship seemed more like mother and son.

She opened her mouth to ask her questions, but he leaned to brush a kiss across her cheek and turned away. Her nerve was lost, and all she felt was relief.

"Come down when you are ready." He closed the door and left her to wash and change.

Even though she took her time, she was downstairs before the sun had dropped below the horizon. It had been a long day, yet curiosity and nerves had her mind and body buzzing.

She found Josiah in the dining room, stacking books. It was a dark room with cobwebs in the corners. He gave her a sheepish look.

"Much like yourself, books were the only things I took from my family home when it was sold."

"And your parents?" Her shoulders tensed to think of Josiah as alone in the world as she was.

"Alive and well and living in a cottage by the sea. The air helps my mother's breathing."

She relaxed. "That sounds lovely. Do you see them often?"

"Not as often as I wish, but we shall go at the first opportunity. My mother will be well pleased I am married." He tapped the stack of books. "Are you hungry? We did not have luncheon."

Her stomach was in such turmoil, she couldn't distinguish hunger from nerves. "Yes, let's eat."

The kitchen table was sturdy and worn, and the room itself warm and homey. "This is lovely. There's no need to clean out the dining room. We can continue to eat in here."

As he doled out the bowls of stew, he said, "I'm afraid we'll be expected to entertain at least occasionally. Lord Marsden's estate backs up to the vicarage. He is our benefactor, at least in part."

"I didn't realize that." The skies were darkening, but she could make out the copse and hints of the field beyond, but no large manor house.

He set the bowls and sliced bread and butter on the table, taking the seat diagonally opposite to her, his knee bumping hers. "He is rarely home, preferring to enjoy all London has to offer, but there are other landowners and villagers who will expect to meet you soon."

"And if they are disappointed?" She poked at the stew with her spoon.

He took her hand and squeezed it. "They won't be, but let's not worry about what tomorrow might bring."

What was that supposed to mean? Did she have to worry about tonight instead? Afraid of the answer, she did not ask the questions scrolling through her head. The stew was as delicious as it smelled, but she could only finish half. Josiah used bread to wipe his bowl clean.

They talked of the village and he told stories about the more colorful members of his flock. The laughter helped ease her nerves until a portent silence fell between them.

"I will take a glass of port in the sitting room if you'd like to prepare yourself," he said without meeting her gaze.

Prepare herself? Was she to be a sacrifice? She rose and moved toward the stairs like an automaton. For a moment, she had a wild notion to open the door and keep walking, but she had made her bed, as her mother would say, and now she must lie in it. A panicked giggled escaped her at the apt platitude.

The room was cooling fast with no fire stoked in the grate. The shadows were long, and she fumbled herself out of her dress and underthings, leaving her in only her thin chemise. The bed loomed like a cave with its dark hangings.

She clambered under the covers and tugged the sheets up so she peeked over. A deep breath settled her. The sheets were crisp and smelled sweet. Better than the cheroot-tinged bedding of the Lyon's Den.

Of course, everything in the Lyon's Den was tinged by the smell of tobacco and liquor. She stretched her legs like a starfish she had seen in one of her books. The size of the bed was decadent. Three times the width of the cot she had tossed and turned in for the last two weeks.

She closed her eyes. The call of a nightbird sounded outside her window. It had probably just woken to hunt at dusk. The rising crescendo of insects pulsed. She had missed the noises of the country while at the Lyon's Den. It was comforting and the one familiar thing she clung to in the uncertainty of the moment.

Could she be happy here? Not just in Upper Wexham, but with Josiah?

And what about him? Could she make him happy, or would she be a disappointment? She had no experience in wifely duties, including the one he expected of her this night.

Noises from downstairs tensed her muscles. Her straining ears could just make out the sound of his footfalls on the stairs. The door opened, startling her, even though she was expecting it. Holding a candle, he loomed in the doorway in shirtsleeves and with damp hair. He carried with him the fresh scent of soap and night air.

His thoughtfulness in bathing didn't surprise her, but she was grateful for it nonetheless. Having grown up with two brothers, she was well acquainted with their smells and habits.

"Hello," she said dumbly for the lack of a better greeting.

"Are you frightened?" His voice had dropped in timbre.

A shiver coursed through her, but she couldn't identify the source. Was she frightened or excited? "Should I be?"

He closed the door behind him and stepped to the edge of the bed, setting the candle on the bedside table. Without preamble or warning, he stripped off his shirt and tossed it aside. "Maybe."

CHAPTER FIVE

AMELIA WASN'T SURE what shocked her more, the muscled expanse of his bare chest or the honesty of his answer. She clutched the covers tighter even as a dry laugh escaped.

"You could at least offer some comforting words even if they aren't true," she said. "You promised I would enjoy what is to come."

His hands dropped to the fastenings of his trousers. "Some women enjoy the marriage bed and some do not."

"Perhaps it is the failure of the man if his wife does not enjoy her duty," she said tartly.

"I agree, and I will do my best to make sure you do not view our intimacies as a duty. However, based on our combustibility at the Lyon's Den, I can safely predict you will enjoy yourself." He paused before adding, "After a moment of discomfort."

"You are not setting my nerves at ease. Do you know what to do or not?"

"I think I can muddle through." He pushed his trousers off and stood before her nude. His staff was at eyelevel. It was a strange looking thing. It stuck straight out from a thatch of hair, the slight tracing of veins visible. The length was less shocking than its girth. It was thick, and the end was mushroom shaped and large. As she stared, a bead of moisture appeared from the slit at the tip.

"That is your cock," she managed to choke out.

His low laugh contained surprise. "Where did you—never mind. The Lyon's Den offered quite an education."

She pushed herself up on her elbows. "And you will push your cock inside of me?"

"That is my intention, yes." His amusement was poorly masked.

"I do not appreciate being laughed at. This is all new to me."

"I'm not laughing at you. I simply never thought to be having such a conversation with a woman. Especially a wife."

"Should I not ask questions? Would you prefer I lie here and let you do what you wish to me?"

"No! Ask me anything. I find it . . . highly arousing." His cock seemed to pulse without him touching it.

"Will it hurt when you put it inside of me? Is that why I should be frightened?"

"It might be uncomfortable the first time."

"Only the first?"

"Once your maidenhead is gone, there is no more pain. From what I've heard. To be frank, I've never been with a virgin."

He wrapped his hand around his cock and casually stroked himself. There was nothing casual about her body's reaction to his actions. Her core ached, and she fought the urge to press her hand between her legs.

"But you have been with many other women? You are a vicar." She tried not to sound accusatory, but something that resembled jealousy pricked her feelings.

"I was not always a vicar, and I wouldn't say I've been with *many* women. A few. Enough to teach me what I like."

"And what do you like?"

"I like your boldness for one thing." He grabbed the covers and swept them away from her body.

Even though she still wore her chemise, she felt exposed and suddenly shy. He lay beside her, his head propped in his hand so he could gaze upon her.

"I'm not feeling very bold at the moment. I would like to huddle under the covers."

"I like your honesty too." A smile flashed across his face. He trailed his fingertips across her cheek, down her neck, and to the ribbon ties at the neckline of her chemise. "My body is yours to explore. You are free to do whatever you wish to satisfy your curiosity."

What she was most curious about, of course, was his cock. He had already demonstrated how to touch it. Shifting slightly, she reached for him, her fingers grazing the tip of his cock. It was damp on the end, but what was even more surprising was the velvety softness of the skin considering what a blunt instrument it appeared to be. She gripped him and stroked from the wiry hair of his pubis to the flanged end. His hips bucked and a hum of satisfaction vibrated his chest against her arm.

"Do you like this?" she asked.

"Too much so. I don't wish to spend in your hand." He pulled her hand up to his mouth and kissed her fingertips. "Perhaps another time."

Another time? Her mind whirled around the possibilities, but the tug on the ribbon holding her chemise together distracted her.

She clutched his forearm. "I assumed I would stay clothed."

"Why did you think that?"

"The girls at the Lyon's Den said the men usually push their skirts up and . . ." Her voice trailed off.

"Fuck them?" He raised his eyebrows. She didn't sense disapproval, but amusement.

"Yes. That's the word they used."

"Perhaps one day I will come upon you in the kitchen or the sitting room, push your skirts up, and fuck you, but tonight, I wish to see you and touch you without hindrance. And I wish to offer myself to you in the same way. Is that acceptable?"

She nodded, unable to work her tongue properly to form words. He freed her arms and pushed the top down until it was gathered around her waist. The light of the candle flickered across the expanse of her flesh.

Her breasts quivered with her quickened shuddery breaths. Never had she been exposed like this. His hungry gaze quashed the urge to cover herself. His eyes were hooded, but his mouth had softened.

"You have ripened into a beautiful woman, Amelia."

Her form was still lean, but her breasts, when they finally budded, had grown round and full. She had viewed them as an annoyance during her treks across the countryside or dodging the lascivious stares of James's friends, but now she found herself arching her back seeking his approval.

He cupped her breast and squeezed gently but firmly. The sensation was shocking and drew forth a gasp.

"Do you like that?" His lips were close to her ear, his hot breath inciting another bolt of lightning.

Her nipples drew into points, but she was not chilled. In fact, she was hot. Very hot.

He pinched her nipple. She threw her head back and bit her lip in a failed attempt to keep a moan at bay.

"Ah, you like that very much." He continued to squeeze her breasts and pinch her nipples while he claimed her mouth in a kiss.

It began as a kiss of domination, but Amelia wasn't overwhelmed for long. Their tongues sparred and danced until they were both breathless, and she squirmed against him. He broke away from her to move his mouth to her breast.

Her breath froze. His tongue flicked at her nipple before taking a nip at the tender point with his teeth. It was intensely pleasurable although she couldn't say why. Of course, the upstairs girls had talked about how gentlemen were enamored of women's breasts, but Amelia didn't understand the pleasure she would experience through his attention.

While he sucked at her breasts, he worked her chemise over her hips, and she kicked it off, no longer harboring any trepidation about being naked. It felt natural and good with him, like Adam and Eve.

He slipped his hand between her thighs. A flitting thought to close her legs evaporated when his finger stroked over her tender flesh.

"You are very responsive to my touch." Satisfaction warmed his voice, and his cock pulsed against her hip. "You like this?"

"Yes," she murmured. "Do you like it?"

"Very much. So much I hope I last long enough to please you."

She wasn't exactly sure what he meant, but her question vanished from her head when he slipped through her wetness to push a finger inside of her.

"Your body is begging for my cock." His lips brushed the shell of her ear and incited shivers even as her body grew even hotter. How was that possible?

She grabbed his forearm, not sure if she wanted to pull his hand away or shove his finger deeper. As curious as Amelia had claimed to be, she had never explored her body this way. His thumb pressed and rubbed at a bundle of nerves that she realized was the apex of her arousal.

Fighting the feeling only grew her frustration. The only way forward was surrender. Did she trust Josiah? Perhaps not in all things, but in this she did. She let go of his arm and raised her hands above her head. A second finger joined the first to stroke inside of her while his thumb continued its work. She closed her eyes and let him guide her toward what her body craved.

A wave lifted her until she dropped into a chasm of pleasure. She cried out and bucked against his hand. His movements slowed until she emerged on the other side, transformed and grateful.

The bed shifted, and her legs were pushed farther apart. She blinked her eyes open, curious as to what would happen next. He was on his knees between her thighs, guiding his cock to her slick opening. Any virginal fear had been incinerated by her climax, and she lifted her hips to meet him. The flanged head of his cock pushed inside of her, the stretch uncomfortable but not unwelcome.

"This is the part that might hurt," he said through clenched teeth.

She gasped at the slight pinch, but the sensation was nothing compared to the feel of him moving deeper inside of her until his hips were seated against her. He gripped her thighs, his fingers trembling. She could sense his control fraying, and a rush of power filled her with satisfaction. She wiggled her hips and was awarded with a groan from him.

"Are you well?" His words slurred together as if intoxicated.

"Better than well. What's next?" Still basking in the aftermath of her own pleasure, she couldn't contain her eagerness to learn more.

He choked out a laugh. Instead of answering her with words, he drew back until just the tip of his cock was inside of her. Before she could protest, he pushed back inside of her with more force this time.

Her breath caught, and she was lost in the sensation. He released her thighs and moved over her, catching her wrists and pressing them over her head. Where she had felt powerful before, now she was at his mercy as he thrust himself in and out of her. Yet, instead of wishing for escape, she submitted willingly to his dominance.

His chest brushed against her nipples. The rough hair against her most sensitive of flesh had her back arching as if making an offering. He gentled the moment with a kiss. The connection between them, both physical and emotional, was undeniable.

A build to pleasure she recognized coiled between her legs, but before she could nurture the feeling, he drove into her one last time and held still. His cock pulsed. He loosened his hold around her wrists and let his forehead fall against her neck.

She ran her hands over his bare shoulders and back, tracing the ridges of muscles. He shivered at her touch. Once more, the power dynamics had shifted. She tightened her knees around his hips and hooked her feet around the back of his thighs, tugging him closer.

He propped himself on his elbows, fingers tangling in her hair to gaze down at her. The candle guttered, and shadows moved over his solemn face. He looked sad, and she couldn't abide it. She kissed him, playfully nipping his bottom lip to get a response. His mouth curved into a slight smile.

He broke away, rolling off her to lay at her side. "Give me a moment to get my legs back, and I'll bring you a cloth."

She pulled the coverlet over her body. Not only was she chilled without his body close, but she was suddenly very aware of her lack of even a nightrail. He was still breathing as if he'd raced up the stairs.

"The deed is done. In olden days, witnesses were required for the act. Sometimes, the bloodied sheet was displayed as evidence of lost virginity." She knew she was babbling yet couldn't stop herself. "I would guess it wasn't always a maiden's blood on the sheet but a freshly killed animal. Have I left a mess?"

She looked down at herself, shifting to see the sheet underneath, but no stain was visible.

"I won't display our sheet for the village, I promise." There was laughter in his voice. He slipped off the bed and retrieved a freshly wrung out cloth from the wash stand.

She propped herself on her elbows to watch him. He was completely unselfconscious in his nakedness. She hadn't had the chance to properly admire or explore his form. There would be another chance soon, she hoped.

She stared at the bed hangings overhead like the darkest of night skies as he cleaned between her legs. She hadn't felt awkward when he'd touched her there before or when he had driven himself inside of her, but the heat of embarrassment his ministration was kindling could set the bed on fire.

"I'm fine. Thank you." She pushed his hand away and tucked the cover around her. What would happen now? The men at the Lyon's Den partaking in the upstairs activities left after the deed, and the women readied themselves for their next customer.

The realities of what the upstairs girls at the Lyon's Den endured settled heavily on her chest. She couldn't imagine welcoming another man into her bed after the intimacy she and Josiah had shared.

He returned the cloth and rejoined her after extinguishing the candles. They lay side-by-side, not touching and silent. His breathing was deep and steady.

She turned on her side to face him, tucking her hands under her cheek, and whispered, "Are you asleep?"

"No." He turned his head in her direction, but with only meager moonlight from the window, she couldn't discern his expression. "Are you well?" His voice was formal.

"Yes and no."

"Did I hurt you?" He shifted to face her, his hand cupping her cheek. "I was too rough. I'm so sorry. I was out of control and—"

"No. I enjoyed it immensely. You weren't too rough, and I'm not hurt. I was thinking about the girls at the Lyon's Den. How can they do that night after night with many different men?"

"Ah, well. I would guess they have few choices in life. Perhaps they were turned out at a young age because there wasn't enough food, or they became orphaned. Survival is a strong instinct. At least, the girls at the Lyon's Den have a room and a bed and plenty of food. Say what you will of Mrs. Dove-Lyon, but she protects the girls against unsavory predilections."

"What sort of predilections?" Her imagination was galloping ahead.

"Some men like to hurt the women they are with or humiliate

them. Some want the women to humiliate them. Some require unnatural things in order to reach their climax. I'm not sure this is a proper discussion to be having with your vicar husband on our wedding night." His amusement ruined his attempt at priggishness.

"Pish-posh. You are not an overly pious vicar."

His hand roamed from her cheek to her bare back, his fingertips tracing the line of her spine. "What do you imagine a pious vicar would have done tonight?"

"I would imagine a pious vicar would have left my nightrail on and blown the candles out."

"Is that what you would have preferred?"

Flames swept through her when she considered what they had done. "Definitely not."

"Then it's a good thing I'm neither pious nor saintly." He kissed her with enough force and passion to kindle her arousal. He pulled away and took a deep breath. "But I'm not entirely without merit as a vicar. I do possess a strong streak of justice."

"That's a more admirable trait for a vicar than the ability to spout off verses." She snuggled into Josiah.

He tugged her closer until her cheek was resting on his arm, and her leg was caught between his. She squeezed her eyes shut to keep unexpected tears from leaking out. For the first time since her brother and parents had died, she felt protected and not alone in the world.

It was too early to say true happiness was within reach, but trust had blossomed between them.

CHAPTER SIX

THE CALL OF an owl brought Josiah out of his light sleep. He almost convinced himself he'd imagined it when it came again. The timing couldn't have been worse. It was his wedding night, and for the first time since he could remember, he wanted to shirk his duties and stay pressed against a very naked Amelia.

His body stirred, and he fought the urge to roll her to her stomach and take her again. But even if the signal hadn't come, she was—or had been—a virgin, and he didn't want to hurt her more than he had already.

Very carefully, he disentangled their limbs and slipped out of bed. Like an angry kitten, she mewled in discontent before snuggling into his pillow. He pulled the covers over her bare shoulders.

Even the chill air couldn't dampen his ardor. He dressed and tip-toed down the stairs in his stockinged feet, avoiding the creaks of the old vicarage. He had learned how to move quickly and silently while in the army serving Wellington. He had tried to leave subterfuge behind after Waterloo, but his job wasn't done—it might never be done—even though he'd sold his commission and taken up the cloth.

A man dressed in black with a low-brimmed hat emerged from the shadows of a willow when he opened the door. He was inside before Josiah could speak a word of warning. The man took off his hat and cloak and made his way into the sitting room to pour himself a glass of brandy from the sideboard.

"Sorry to wake you, Barrymore. I'm not alone. A friend is huddling by a gravestone and chanting prayers to keep the ghosts away. We need to see him settled."

Josiah shushed him while coaxing the embers in the grate into a fire. "I'm not alone either. You must be quiet."

Sir Gray Masterson's eyebrows lifted. "You have a woman in your bed? That's a risky proposition considering your calling."

"Actually, I have a wife in my bed. I was wed yesterday."

Sir Gray choked on a sip of his brandy, doing his best to muffle the noise. Eyes watering, he finally got words out. "Why wasn't I informed?"

"Terribly sorry, I didn't realize I needed your approval, sir." His whispered apology dripped with insincerity and sarcasm.

"Not approval perhaps, but this could certainly complicate matters." Sir Gray paced in front of the hearth and rubbed at his forehead.

"You might congratulate me." Josiah perched on the arm of a chair.

"Of course, congratulations." Sir Gray paused, his eyes narrowing. "But you can't deny it was sudden. Who is she? Can she be trusted?"

"You see enemies in every shadow. The last I heard we are no longer at war."

Sir Gray snorted. "Don't try to sell me that balderdash. The game is always afoot even if we don't have soldiers on the field."

Josiah couldn't argue the point considering he was still working for Sir Gray Masterson and the Home Office. "I married Miss Amelia Fielding."

Sir Gray stilled and turned to face Josiah. "Daniel Fielding's sister?"

"The very same."

"That's a development I never anticipated." Which was saying something since Sir Gray survived by anticipating every eventuality. "I assume you had a good reason to marry in haste?"

"Her surviving brother James is a blackguard and has been making things difficult for her."

"Well." Sir Gray took a seat and stared into the flames. After a long moment, he asked softly, "Will you tell her the truth?"

"I don't see how I can keep it a secret for long."

"I don't like it."

"I don't either, but I couldn't leave Amelia at the mercy of her brother. I owe it to Daniel to protect his sister." Josiah slid his gaze to meet the intensity of Sir Gray's green stare. "And so do you."

"Perhaps so." Gray rubbed at his chin. "You must do your best to keep your feelings detached. She could become your weakness."

Josiah was at a loss for a response, and when he didn't immediately answer, Sir Gray shot him a piercing look and cursed. "It's already too late, isn't it?"

"I barely know the chit." Even Josiah didn't believe his weak denial.

Sir Gray merely shook his head and glanced toward the ceiling. "Where shall we stow our informant until Hanson can collect him?"

"Why can't you transport him yourself?" Josiah wasn't sure exactly where the German would be taken until all information was squeezed out of him, but he had assumed London or nearby.

"My wife would have my head if I turned up with him at the town house. In any case, we are due to travel to Wintermarsh to greet our new niece, and our German friend is headed the opposite direction from London."

"In that case, the vestry will have to do."

"It will only be until tomorrow. Surely you can keep him out of sight for that long?"

"You're lucky it's not Sunday. Even so, I'm expecting the ladies of the Upper Wexham to queue up to visit once word gets around that I married."

Sir Gray tossed back his glass of spirits and set it down empty. "What's your sermon about this week?"

"No idea. I haven't written it yet, but perhaps it should be about the danger of secrets," Josiah said wryly.

Sir Gray muffled a laugh on his way out the door and into the night to retrieve his informant.

After pulling on his boots, Josiah paused and glanced up the stairs toward the bedchamber, but he could hear no movement. His sigh of relief was followed by worry. He would have to decide how to handle the situation soon. Amelia was bright and curious and wouldn't be fooled for long. But for tonight, at least, Josiah could avoid the difficult decision.

He and Sir Gray got the man settled in the vestry. The German hadn't stopped his liturgy the entire time. Josiah hoped he could calm his nerves enough to be silent. Otherwise, drugged tea would be served in the morning. Josiah couldn't risk one of the village ladies wandering in to pray and hearing a man gibbering away in a foreign language.

Josiah looked away from the man propped into the corner of the vestry, partially hidden by the robes. The fear on the man's face settled an anger in Josiah's belly that would not grant him a benediction. Or maybe the God from the Old Testament would approve.

After Josiah shut and locked the door, he asked, "What information does the man carry?"

"He's a minor noble of one of the states that were swallowed up in the formation of the German Confederation. His father attempted to foment a rebellion to reclaim their land and titles. It failed, of course. The father died, but his son was privy to meetings with the heads of other small Germanic states in the same situation. We are hoping to determine any principalities at risk."

"Obviously, further rebellions could destabilize the entire region."

"The German Confederation has been heavily influenced by Napoleon's egalitarian ideals."

"Is that such a bad thing?" Josiah would never voice the opinion in front of anyone else, but Sir Gray had not always been a "sir." He had been born a commoner. And the excesses of England's king were legendary.

"Not when it spreads peacefully, but the risk of war is ever present. The heads of these disbanded German states feel slighted, and they still hold power and sway over their people."

"The people will be better off without royalty draining their livelihoods. Why can't they realize it?"

"England will try to help them shed the bonds of their monarchies."

Josiah huffed a laugh that was dry and humorless. "Ironic that we are promoting exactly what Napoleon was preaching amongst everyone but our own people."

Sir Gray shrugged, but his eyes were shadowed and uneasy. "The longer I dabble in foreign affairs, the more I come to understand how nuanced and muddled it can become. In a way, war is easy. It's simple to recognize who is your enemy when you are facing off on opposite sides of a battlefield. Kill or be killed."

"You are starting to sound bitter. Are you ready to retire to the country and become a gentleman farmer?"

"Not as long as I feel I can still do good. What about yourself? Does this marriage change your mindset? Do you want out?"

"Not as long as I feel I can still do good," Josiah mimicked.

Sir Gray flipped the collar on his greatcoat up and pulled his hat lower. "I'll be getting on. Expect Hanson."

Josiah did not like Hanson even though the man had done nothing over the last two years to betray them. "Why do you trust him?"

Sir Gray pressed himself to the side of the church door and

checked outside with a quick, sweeping glance. Only the dead kept them company this night. "I don't trust anyone, Barrymore. Not even you. Hanson can be . . . problematic, but he has valuable contacts in the seediest areas of London. What he offers outweighs the risks. At the moment."

If that changed, Sir Gray would cut Hanson loose, and he would probably turn up drowned in the Thames. The sobering fact was that the same could happen to Josiah.

With the unsaid warning hanging in the air, Sir Gray disappeared between gravestones, the rising fog swirling around his legs.

After delivering water from the well and a hunk of Mrs. Drinkwater's fruitcake for his unexpected guest, Josiah climbed up the stairs to his wife.

His wife. The unexpected twists of life never failed to shock him. He should have died ten times over in Portugal or Spain. Daniel had been the more careful of the two of them. Double and triple checking his contacts and the security of his meeting spots. Josiah had taken unnecessary risks and invited death to try to take him.

Only after Daniel had been stabbed trying to help a Spanish woman who had preyed on his gentlemanly impulses did Josiah understand the fragility of life. He had also learned that trust had to be earned.

Even though she was his wife, Amelia had not earned his trust. He would keep his secrets. For now.

He undressed and slipped back into bed. She rolled toward him and cuddled into his side. His blood quickened.

"Why are you so cold?" she asked in a sleepy voice.

"I heard a noise and went outside to investigate." He was proud of himself for not lying to her.

Her breasts were soft against him. He wouldn't take her again, but he allowed himself to draw her closer and run his hand up and down the silky skin of her back. His thoughts traversed his worries. His new wife. The man in the vestry. Writing his next sermon. Avoiding lightning striking him down in the pulpit.

A smile turned his lips. How many times had he found himself smiling or even laughing today? More than the entire past year put together. Considering what Amelia had been through the last weeks, she could have been cowed and fearful or bitter and angry. Instead, she had showed admirable bravery in the face of the unknown.

While they weren't complete strangers, she must have been anxious about sharing his bed after reacquainting themselves just that morning. If the indelible memories of entering her tight wet heat weren't still fresh, he might question the encounter. But her passion had been real. As had his.

In a moment of clarity, he realized Gray was right. She could become his weakness. Maybe she already was. The thought of someone hurting her set his blood afire. She had been through enough, first losing Daniel and her parents, and then betrayed by James, who should have protected her.

It was his job now. Josiah would make sure nothing could hurt Amelia, even if that meant keeping his secrets.

CHAPTER SEVEN

AMELIA WOKE WITH a delicious sense of contentment. She stretched and the covers slipped to her waist. Cool air tickled her bare skin. Her senses were newly awakened, and even as she smiled, a blush suffused her face. Never had she thought the intimacies shared in the marriage bed would be so . . . well, *intimate*.

She rose and dressed herself in a simple day gown of light blue with green sprigs. The neckline was scooped but modest. Was it modest enough for a vicar's wife? Just in case, she tied a white fringed shawl around her shoulders before going downstairs.

Never could she have imagined herself in such circumstances. It seemed unreal. The smell of bread baking brought her back to reality. Her stomach growled. Even though the vicarage was her home now, she hesitated on entering the kitchen.

Mrs. Drinkwater was behind that door, and Amelia wasn't confident of her welcome. She had never been a ninny or a coward, and she wouldn't start now. With more bravado than bravery, she marched to the kitchen and pushed the door open.

Mrs. Drinkwater pulled a pan of sweet rolls out of the large black oven and set them atop a cooling rack. "Ah, there you are. Good morning, Mrs. Barrymore. The vicar has gone to tend to his flock. I took the liberty of making you a plate."

Mrs. Drinkwater lifted a linen napkin to reveal a plate piled with sausage and eggs. From the sideboard, she retrieved toast and a small helping of red jam.

"Thank you, Mrs. Drinkwater. I am famished." Still, Amelia hesitated to seat herself. "I understand my arrival was unexpected. Actually, the entire series of events yesterday was unexpected for me as well. While I would like to claim I have experience running a household, I fear that would be a lie. And I suppose as a vicar's wife, I should try to avoid those."

She forced a strained laugh out. While Mrs. Drinkwater didn't so much as favor her with a warm smile, something about her demeanor seemed to soften, although perhaps that was wishful thinking on Amelia's part.

"I wasn't planning on leaving you high and dry, missus. Now, sit and eat."

Was Mrs. Drinkwater's tone a bit dictatorial for a housekeeper to her mistress? Perhaps, but Amelia decided now was not the time to assert her meager authority. After all, if Mrs. Drinkwater quit, Amelia would be left to burn toast and beans for their dinner.

Amelia dug in with gusto and nearly cleaned her plate before pushing back. "That was delicious. I would like to learn to cook if you are patient enough to teach me."

"I would be happy to." Mrs. Drinkwater paused and added unexpectedly, "I was widowed young. My husband was lost at sea, and my only son marched to war to become cannon fodder. Mr. Barrymore reminds me of my son very much, and I suppose I regard him as family now. I would very much like to stay on."

Amelia understood what it was to be alone and adrift in the world. It was difficult for women without a father or husband or brother to survive in the world. She put her hand to her chest and gave a tremulous smile. "Of course. I will need all the help I can get. And I hope you will come to regard me as part of your family, too."

Mrs. Drinkwater's mouth tightened, and she turned away to the sink.

Not sure if the woman was pleased or annoyed, Amelia backed toward the door. "I believe I will explore a bit."

Once she was outside, Amelia took a deep breath and looked around. The fog was still thick as the sun remained in hiding behind low-slung gray clouds. She shivered, not from cold, but the eeriness of the gravestones reaching out of the fog.

Was Josiah in the church? She wanted to see him. What she craved most was reassuring words after their wedding night. Had she pleased him? What did he expect from her going forward? Would it be unseemly to request they perform the act again tonight?

She picked her way through the graveyard. The church was narrow with a tall steeple. The bell appeared weather-beaten but in good condition. The white clapboard was clean and the walk leading to the front was lined with rose bushes. It was lovely.

She stepped inside and was met with total silence. She searched for peace in the eerily quiet space, but instead, the hairs on the back of her neck quivered.

There was no sign of Josiah. Tending to his flock could mean many different things. He might be in the village visiting the sick or needy. She wandered to the front of the church and looked up at the pulpit where Josiah would give his sermon come Sunday. She had a difficult time picturing him as a vicar.

A bang came from the back of the church and made her start. A heavy curtain in the corner drew her closer. She pushed it to the side, surprised to find a door. Pressing her ear against the cool wood, she listened, but heard nothing more. It could have been a mouse.

"Josiah? Is that you?" Uncertainty made her voice creak.

A fist rapped on the door, and she stumbled backward, her heart hammering in her chest. That was no mouse on the other side. And it wasn't Josiah either. Whoever it was spoke a foreign language.

She calmed down enough to listen to what he was saying. She picked a few words out here and there. The only thing she was sure of was that he was German. Unfortunately, she was much better at reading than conversing German, but she was fairly certain the man was asking for help. Had he somehow become stuck? Was he a traveler seeking refuge in the church?

The man's voice contained no anger, just desperation tinged with sadness. Amelia's heart went out to him. She had experienced the same when she'd run away from James to land at the Lyon's Den.

She would take the man to Josiah. He would know what to do. The door handle turned, but the door did not open. Amelia squatted down and found the problem. A piece of wood had become wedged in the mechanism. She tugged it free and the door swung open.

The man on the other side stared at her with wide eyes full of fear. Amelia hoped her smile offered a promise of safety. Tentatively, she tried a few words in the rudimentary German she spoke. *Safety. Food. Husband. Help.*

Her attempt at his language seemed to offer comfort. He approached and took her hands, speaking too quickly for her to understand. She tried to tell him to slow down, but he seemed desperate to impart his message. She glanced down and realized he was pressing a piece of folded parchment into her hands. The red wax seal was crumbling, and the paper was lined with deep creases.

Was it a letter? Did he want her to post it? She turned it over but there was no direction written on the paper. Before she could ask him anymore, the door burst open at the front of the church. Out of instinct, she backed into the room with the man.

Josiah was out of breath, his cheeks ruddy. He stopped short when he spotted her in the room with the man. He slowed his approach as if not wanting to spook a wild animal, his hands up, his footfalls silent.

"Come out of there, Amelia." His voice was soft and soothing.

She glanced over her shoulder. The German was cowering in the corner, his fear palpable. His fear infected her. She wasn't scared of Josiah, but whatever was going on had taken on a sinister air. She slipped the letter into a pocket in her skirts and didn't move. "What's going on?"

"Nothing you need to concern yourself with." Josiah was blocking the doorway now.

"I feel concerned. Very concerned. This man is obviously afraid. He is also German. He was stuck. The vestry door was jammed closed."

His glance over her shoulder and hesitation clued her in.

"You locked him in, didn't you?" Disbelief sailed her voice high.

"I did, but for his own good. He can't be wandering about the village."

Realization hit her like a punch. "This is what you were dealing with last night, isn't it? You said you heard a noise."

"I did hear a noise."

She narrowed her eyes on him. "Are you a smuggler?"

The corner of his mouth twitched the tiniest bit. "No."

"Are you involved in anything that could get you hanged?"

He seemed to consider the question. "Not in England."

Anger superseded her fear. She set her fists on her hips. "You'll tell me what's going or you can lock me in the vestry too."

Josiah sighed and rubbed his face. Exhaustion was etched around his eyes, but Amelia refused to let sympathy take root. If he wasn't lying to her, he was certainly not telling her the entire truth.

"Are you even a vicar?" she whispered.

"Yes. Not a very good one though. Will you please come out? That man could hurt you." He made a "come here" gesture with his fingers, his hand outstretched.

"Don't be ridiculous. He's harmless."

"How can you possibly know that?"

"For one thing, he could have bashed me over the head with one of those big crosses on the wall and run away before you even arrived. For another, his hands are very soft. Obviously, he's used to a certain standard that probably doesn't include sleeping on a vestry floor. Or bashing people over the head. He is a gentleman on the run and more afraid than anything."

Josiah let his arms drop to the side in a gesture of frustrated capitulation. "What would you have me do with him?"

"Let's take him back to the vicarage and offer him tea. I speak a bit of German, you know."

"I didn't know actually."

"I'm fluent in French and Spanish. I tried to learn Russian, but it was very difficult."

"You are a woman of many talents. I should have known." Josiah stepped back. "Can you tell the German he is invited for tea?"

"I can try." And she did try with halting words and hand gestures. The man nodded but moved with obvious trepidation. Amelia caught up with Josiah who was moving quickly to the door. "What about Mrs. Drinkwater?"

"What about her?" Josiah checked for witnesses before leading them out of the church.

"Will she be surprised you are hosting a foreigner for tea?"

"She is discreet."

"In other words, this is not the first time. Is she involved?" Amelia asked. "And why didn't you involve me?"

"I hardly planned for this to happen on our wedding night. Anyway, I wasn't sure if . . ." He shrugged, and she stopped in the middle of the graveyard.

"If what?" She grabbed the sleeve of his jacket and forced him to face her.

"If you can be trusted. Can you?" His gaze was pointed and eviscerating.

"I don't even know what you are not trusting me with so it's difficult to answer that question."

Josiah rubbed his brow as if a headache was brewing. "Let's get inside before someone sees us and starts asking questions."

The German trailed after them into the house. Mrs. Drinkwater came out of the kitchen, wiping her hands on her apron only to come to a dead stop. Her gaze darted between the three of them. "What's going on?"

"Amelia stumbled over our guest. Could you bring a tea tray to the sitting room?"

It was obvious Mrs. Drinkwater did not like the turn of events, but she turned to do Josiah's bidding. With his demeanor guarded, the German sat gingerly on the edge of the armchair.

Amelia didn't want to make him any more skittish than he already was. She smiled and nodded at him before directing her ire toward her husband. "What are you mixed up in? Is it dangerous?"

"It's not usually dangerous." He stood to the side of the window and flicked the curtain aside to see the front walk.

"But it can be dangerous." She was beginning to tease out the true meanings behind his answers. "How long will the German be with us?"

"His escort should be arriving any time."

"And where will he be escorted?" Once more, Amelia sent a warm, reassuring smile to the German, but he still looked tensely back and forth between them, and she wondered how much he might understand.

"London for questioning, and then somewhere safe."

"Questioning by whom?"

"Can we discuss this later, Amelia?"

She stomped her foot, smashing any pretense of warmth and welcome for the German's benefit. "No, we will discuss it now. I will not allow you to hand him over to ruffians to be abused."

"Firstly, he's not a puppy. He's a man with valuable information who has fled his homeland and is seeking asylum. There are well-placed men in our government who are interested in that information and have the means to protect him."

"You are working for the Crown?" The notion helped settle her ruffled feathers a bit.

"I work for the same organization that Daniel and I worked for during the war."

Her ire rose again. "The one that got my brother killed?"

Josiah opened and closed his mouth without speaking before finally saying, "Yes. Although, it is not as dangerous as it was during the war."

"How often should I expect visitors?" She gestured toward the German, then tapped her forehead with her palm. "The room upstairs is outfitted for such occasions, isn't it? And Mrs. Drinkwater is well aware and even helps, doesn't she?"

"I do," Mrs. Drinkwater said from the doorway. She appeared untroubled and deposited the tray on the table closest to the German. She poured him a cup and the man took it with a word of thanks.

"He said thank you," Amelia offered as she received a cup from Mrs. Drinkwater as well.

"He's very welcome." Mrs. Drinkwater took up her own cup instead of leaving them. "After my son died, I felt helpless. Working with Mr. Barrymore has given me a purpose. It makes me feel as if my son did not die in vain."

Mrs. Drinkwater's voice cracked at the end, and Amelia couldn't help but offer comfort. She put her hand on Mrs. Drinkwater's forearm and squeezed but didn't linger, not sure how the housekeeper would receive the familiarity.

"I do understand," Amelia said softly.

"I believe you do." Mrs. Drinkwater and Amelia seemed to come to an understanding in that moment. They were two women buffeted by war and fate to accept situations out of their control.

Muffled feminine chatter carried up the walk. Josiah peeked out the window and muffled a curse. "It's Mrs. Hamilton and her daughters. We can't receive them. Not right now."

Mrs. Drinkwater set her cup down with a clatter and smoothed the apron over her skirts. "Let me handle them. Be quiet and stay away from the window."

Mrs. Drinkwater went outside to greet the women on the front path. When the German started to ask a question, Amelia shushed him and stumbled about for the right word for "quiet." She must have landed on something near enough because the German sank back into the chair and sipped his tea.

After five minutes, Mrs. Drinkwater returned. "I told them you and your new wife were out walking behind the vicarage. It seemed to satisfy them, but they'll be back."

"Now that Amelia is aware of the way of things, why don't you show our guest upstairs and allow him to clean up and rest until Hanson arrives," Josiah said.

Amelia waited until she was alone with her husband to speak her heart. "I wish you'd told me before I agreed to marry you."

His eye twitched, but his voice remained even. "Would you have said no?"

"Perhaps. Perhaps not. But I should have been given the chance to decide with all of the information."

"I apologize." He tugged on his collar and looked to the ground. "You are more like your brother than I gave you credit for. I should have trusted you, but I am out of the habit, to be honest."

"How long did you think you could keep me in the dark about your non-clergy-related activities?"

The ghost of a smile crossed his face. "A sight longer than the few hours I managed to. I must be slipping. Can you ever forgive me?"

Amelia heaved a sigh. She was still perturbed at his lie by omission, but she couldn't deny the subterfuge offered excitement beyond the duties of a vicar's wife. "I will forgive you only if you allow me to help."

"But—"

"Mrs. Drinkwater is your ally. Your wife should be your partner."

"I don't want to see you hurt." He came to stand in front of her. "I have a duty to protect you. Daniel would expect it of me."

"Is that the only reason you don't want to see me hurt?"

"Of course not. I sense a growing fondness between us. Can I hope you feel the same?"

"Yes," she whispered.

He wrapped an arm around her waist and pulled her close. "Are you sore from last night?"

Heat suffused her, but she wasn't sure if it was embarrassment from the intimate question or arousal from the feel of his hard body against her. "A tad when I awoke, but it has faded."

He claimed her lips, and she wrapped her arms around his neck. His kisses were skillful and intoxicating. His hands roamed down her back, loosening the tapes of her bodice.

She gasped. "What are you doing?"

"I'm demonstrating my growing fondness for my bride." He slipped a hand to her bottom and pushed his erection against her belly.

His double entendre made her laugh. "I had no idea how large your fondness would grow."

He joined in her laughter and swooped in to claim another kiss.

She stopped him with a firm hand on his chest and tried to sound serious in spite of her breathlessness. "You are trying to distract me from asking questions."

He tilted his head slightly, his eyebrows rising. "Is it working?"

She fought her smile and lost. Never had she thought the act between a man and wife could involve teasing and fun. Of course, her experience was limited to stories from prostitutes in a brothel.

"Yes, but only for now. Don't think that I'll be put off for long." This time she kissed him. Their hands were busy. She pushed his black frockcoat over his shoulders to fall on the floor. Her bodice sagged ever lower, and his lips coasted over the curves of her breasts.

"Are we . . . are you . . . don't we require a bed for the act?" she gasped out.

"I could lift your skirts, press you against the wall, and fuck you. Or lean you over the settee and take you from behind. Or . . ." He led her to the settee and took a seat in the middle.

Before she had to guess what to do, he guided her onto his lap in a straddle. Her skirts were drawn up around her knees. She grabbed the cushioned back of the settee as he worked her bodice to her waist, tugging down her chemise in the process. Her half-stays offered up her breasts to his eyes and mouth. He plucked one and then the other higher to expose her nipples.

He tweaked them both before lowering his mouth to draw one of them in for a strong suck. His eyes were closed, his face suffused with color. It was one thing to be allowing such intimacies in the candle-light, another altogether to be watching him suckle at her breast in the light of day. The pleasure ricocheting through her body overrode her sense of modesty, and she let her head fall back, sinking into the moment.

With fledgling instincts born just last night, she rotated her hips closer. His hands moved to her knees and traveled up her thighs, over her soft lawn drawers to find the split in the middle. He touched the tender flesh between her legs. She dropped her face to his shoulder and bucked even closer, craving the confident touch he had demon-strated last night.

"You're already so wet for me, sweetheart." His warm breath in her ear incited a wave of shivers.

He fumbled with his trousers and pulled her pelvis into his. The hard heat of his cock pressed directly against her.

She fisted her hands in the cushion, her frustration climbing with her arousal. "Tell me what to do."

"You've ridden a horse, yes?" He had a firm grip on her hips and moved her against him, her core sliding along his length with ease.

"Yes, but what do horses have to do with anything?"

"Ride me, Amelia." His whisper was full of dark promises of pleasure. She would have thrown herself off a cliff if he'd told her it would bring her a climax.

He guided the tip of his cock to her folds, and she slowly let her body sink down to take the entire length of him. Like a jockey, he helped her find a rhythm, rising and falling upon him. His breaths were short and fast, and his hands tightened on her hips.

The friction was delicious. She increased her pace, and his groan flooded her with both pleasure and power. She could dictate how fast and hard she rode him. He slipped his hand to her pubis, pressing his fingers against the apex, close to where he was sliding in and out of her.

The extra pressure felt like being thrown from a horse with a suddenness that was shocking. She lost her rhythm, her body pulsing around his cock. Having him inside of her when she climaxed was new and wonderous.

It was his turn to take control, and he raised and lowered her upon him with a savagery that might have shocked her if she hadn't still been riding her own pleasure. With one final stab, he succumbed, his head back, his teeth bared as his spend leaked out of her.

In the aftermath, he nuzzled her breasts, laying gentle kisses along her heated skin, as he righted her bodice. "I'm afraid we need to repair ourselves. There is much we must face today."

The implication of his words settled warmly in her chest. They would face whatever happened next together.

With Herculean effort, she climbed off his lap and tumbled to the corner of the settee. He offered his handkerchief, and she blushed when she realized why. Keeping her gaze averted, she cleaned herself as discreetly as possible before shaking her skirts down and rising. She tucked hair back into her braid and stole glances at him. His trousers were fastened, his jacket back on, and he was straightening his simple cravat.

"Will we often partake in such activities in the middle of the morning?" she asked.

"Did I shock you?" He looked more curious than chagrinned.

"Yes, but not in an unpleasant way. I can't imagine my parents . . ." She shook the thought out of her head. "Is this the way of most marriages?"

Josiah snaked an arm around her and brought her close, brushing his lips over hers. "Society marriages often seem to be made to form alliances either for money or power. I would imagine the marriage bed is not particularly warm or happy in those cases. But in Upper Wexham, I have performed marriages where the woman is already with child. And you and I seem to be combustible." His voice held a note of something she didn't like.

"Are you troubled by this?" She pushed against his chest to force him to meet her gaze.

"It complicates my work. You are a weakness."

She broke his hold on her altogether. "A weakness? An intelligent wife who is not blind to your subterfuge is a weakness? I suppose it would have been easier if I were a ninny who accepted your lies as truths."

He held his hands up and shrugged. "I can't say that's not true."

She balled up her fist as Daniel had taught her and punched him in the shoulder. She was gratified to see his eyes widen in surprise even though she was sure her puny attempt had not hurt him in the least. It had felt like punching rock.

"What I meant was that if an enemy senses that I care for you, he—or she—can use you against me knowing I would do whatever it took to keep you safe." He brushed a lock of escaped hair behind her ear.

"Oh." It was the only response she could muster.

"Hanson will be here soon to collect our German friend. I could use your help to speak with him before I hand him over. Will you help me?"

CHAPTER EIGHT

I T WASN'T IN Josiah's nature to ask anyone for help, but he couldn't deny Amelia had skills he did not. She was intelligent and brave and ... damn, he was getting hard again just thinking about her boldness. He had to at least wait until they retired to bed before fucking her again.

He shouldn't have taken her in the sitting room. Not with a foreigner who might be dangerous upstairs along with half the village gossips lying in wait to question him on his hasty marriage and Hanson ready to show his face at any moment.

Any sense of self-preservation had vanished when he'd come to the open vestry door to find Amelia ready to defend a stranger like a lioness. Her flashing eyes and cutting gaze had aroused him to the point of recklessness.

They had only been married a day. She was practically a stranger, except for their connection through her brother. And yet ... he understood Amelia, maybe better than she understood herself, because they were very alike.

Their exploratory kiss at the Lyon's Den had ignited a passion neither of them could deny. It threatened to burn out of control.

Perhaps it would dim over time, but right now Josiah was having a difficult time concentrating on the matters at hand.

It wasn't merely her beauty that attracted him. It was her strength of mind and character and the ability she possessed to make him smile. And now he watched as she used her ability with languages to question the German.

Through a halting mixture of German and French, Amelia extracted a meager amount of information from their foreign guest. His given name was Heinrich, but he did not offer his family name, probably because it would give away too much. The basic facts seemed to point to a planned coup attempt through the assassination of a high-ranking member of the German Confederation.

What neither France nor England needed was instability on the Continent. The long war had emptied England's coffers and the rank and file would not tolerate more conflict. Too much—and too many— had been lost.

Amelia sat back and blew an escaped tendril of hair off her face. "Heinrich is not going to say more, and even if he did, I'm not sure I would understand the intricacies of the plot."

Mrs. Drinkwater stuck her head in the door. "That man is here."

That man was how Mrs. Drinkwater referred to Hanson. She didn't like or trust him, and Josiah never corrected her, because he felt the same way about the man. Every time he saw Sir Gray, he asked for a new contact, and every time he'd been rebuffed.

For a moment, he considered asking Amelia to retreat to their bedchamber while Hanson was here, but one look at her face erased the idea. Her curiosity had been piqued, and nothing would deny her from taking part in the exchange. Anyway, her ability with the German language, as rudimentary as it was, might prove useful.

Josiah entered the kitchen where Mrs. Drinkwater had parked Hanson with tea and a piece of bread slavered in plum jam. Hanson's gaze went directly to Amelia, his eyes alight with a twinkle that made

Josiah want to punch him. He refrained. Barely.

"The village is all atwitter with your marriage. I thought I might find her already heavy with child. Is that why you wed in haste?" Remaining seated, Hanson grinned and took a big bite out of his bread, chewing with his mouth open. Mastering the social niceties was not high on Hanson's list of skills.

Before Josiah could offer a set-down, Amelia stepped up, her arms akimbo. "Your manners are deplorable, sir, and it's none of your business why we married. Your only job is to see Heinrich safely to where he needs to go."

"Aren't you a bossy little chit?" Hanson shoved the rest of the bread into his mouth and rose.

Showing anger would give Hanson a trump card over him, but Josiah couldn't stop himself. He grabbed Hanson by the shirtfront and jabbed him in the throat. Not hard enough to do damage, but hard enough to make his point. Hanson doubled over searching for breath.

"Once you are able, you may apologize to my wife, Hanson. Then, you can be on your way with your charge." Josiah kept his voice calm.

Hanson set his hands on his knees and looked up at Amelia. "Didn't know Barrymore here could be so sensitive. Sorry, ma'am." He sounded more amused than sorry, but Josiah had already revealed too much of his weakness where Amelia was concerned.

"You're lucky my husband was closer. I would have kicked you between your legs, sirrah." Amelia's sharp tone made Josiah want to smile, but he forced his lips to stay firmly in a frown.

Hanson acknowledged her with a slight tipping of his head. Threats were the only language Hanson spoke fluently.

"How are you traveling?" Josiah asked.

"On foot to a disused barn outside of the village, and then horse-back. The man can ride?"

"I would assume so." If Heinrich was even a minor branch off a royal tree, then he would have grown up riding. "Riding leaves you exposed to sharpshooters."

"Yes, but carriage travel is slow. And the road at least from here to London should be well-traveled—far enough to be sure no one's following."

"Come on, then. He's in the sitting room."

It took a stumbling back-and-forth between Heinrich and Amelia for her to explain the situation. Heinrich did not look happy to be heading off into the unknown with Hanson, but Josiah needed Heinrich and Hanson out of the vicarage. Mrs. Hamilton would only be put off once. She would be back sooner rather than later to set eyes on Amelia. The last thing Amelia needed to be worrying about was a German stashed upstairs while pouring tea and dodging questions about their quick marriage.

Josiah saw the two men out the back door. According to Hanson, they would cut through the woods and fields behind the vicarage before retrieving the two horses Hanson had left in the abandoned barn. As the two men disappeared, Josiah allowed himself a sigh of relief before turning his worries back to the more mundane tasks of receiving visitors.

Mrs. Hamilton and her two unmarried daughters returned not a quarter hour after Hanson and Heinrich departed. There could be no excuse not to receive them this time.

Amelia greeted the trio of ladies with a smile and warm words of welcome. Her hair was still disheveled from their lovemaking on the settee, but otherwise she looked the picture of a vicar's wife. The visitors sat side-by-side on the settee in a flurry of skirts and speculative glances at Josiah and Amelia.

A blush becomingly pinkened Amelia's cheeks. Was she recalling the scorching intimacy that took place on the settee that very morning? He took the armchair across from the settee and assembled the mask he wore when speaking to his flock.

At first, he'd felt disingenuous when attempting to offer words of wisdom or comfort to those in need, but he found his experiences facing hardship and tragedy during the war had equipped him in unexpected ways to tend to the spiritual needs of Upper Wexham. He might not quote Scripture, but he understood loss and could offer true empathy as much as it was worth.

"You could have knocked me down with a feather when I heard the news of your marriage, Mr. Barrymore. Let me be one of the first to offer my congratulations." Before Josiah could thank her, she continued. "Of course, I was disappointed you did not marry one of the girls in Upper Wexham."

Mrs. Hamilton looked pointedly at her older daughter, Patience, a pretty girl without a serious thought in her head. She was always tittering about something or another whether it was warranted or not. Case in point, the young lady had covered her mouth with a lace-gloved hand to stifle giggles.

Her younger sister, Grace, who was by far the most level-headed female in their household didn't bother to hide her eye-roll. He had a feeling Amelia and Grace would get along like wildfire. In fact, they might be dangerous together.

"Mrs. Barrymore's brother and I were friends. I met her when I was a young soldier yet to see battle. Daniel and I bought our commissions together."

Amelia poured tea for them all. Once she had taken her cup and sat back, she added, "I admit to carrying a tendresse for Josiah back then. I thought him quite dashing and handsome in his regimentals."

Mrs. Hamilton took a sip from her cup, her mouth puckering as if it was filled with dirty dishwater. "I'm surprised this brother of yours did not want a proper wedding, Mrs. Barrymore."

"Daniel is dead, ma'am." Amelia's tone stayed sweetly cool. "As are my parents."

Grace shot her mother a sharp look before sitting forward. "The price of war was our brothers, fathers, husbands. My father was one of the first to perish so many years ago."

"I'm sorry we have loss in common." Amelia's expression and tone had softened.

The silence that followed felt full of their collective memories. Josiah had enough ghosts to crush the room. He cleared his throat. "I have no doubt Upper Wexham will welcome Amelia and make her new home comfortable."

For some reason, Patience seemed to find this amusing and covered her mouth to stem another fit of giggles.

Mrs. Hamilton gave a sharp nod as if bestowing her judgement. "The women's auxiliary meets next week. We plan to assemble baskets for the less fortunate in Upper Wexham. You will want to attend, of course, Mrs. Barrymore. We host a summer fete in the village square. I'm sure you will have many pleasing ideas to contribute."

"Yes, indeed," Amelia murmured. Her teacup rattled against the saucer.

Josiah almost smiled. Amelia could escape her conniving brother to land in a gaming hell, marry in haste, and confront a German hideaway without batting an eyelash, but the thought of playing hostess to the village women was leaving her flustered.

But it seemed as if their common losses would be a binding force, and with Mrs. Hamilton's approval, Amelia would have an easier time being accepted by the other women in the village. He stared at Amelia's profile as she continued to make conversation with the Hamiltons.

He wanted her to be happy in Upper Wexham and happy with him. It was a startling thought. How long had it been since he'd been worried about someone else's happiness? How long had it been since he'd felt happiness within his own grasp?

A surge of disquiet streaked through him. What if he couldn't keep her safe? He wasn't worried about her hapless brother, James. Though he was a coward at heart, he might take some convincing to accept Amelia's marriage to Josiah. That convincing might take the form of words or fists. It depended on how desperate James was.

It was the work Josiah did for Sir Gray and the Home Office that posed the biggest risk to Amelia. Would Sir Gray allow him to resign his position in the network? Could Josiah become what the world at large assumed him to be—a simple vicar?

He rose abruptly drawing all the ladies' gazes. "Excuse me. I have my Sunday sermon to write."

While it was true, he doubted he would be able to clear his mind enough to focus. Amelia sent him a questioning look, but he stalked out to stew in his own troubles.

CHAPTER NINE

AMELIA'S SMILE WAVERED as Josiah left the room. The look on his face had been one of worry, but what had prompted his change of mood? She continued to make pleasantries with Mrs. Hamilton and her daughters. Patience was a feather-brain, but Grace was sharp and sarcastic, and Amelia could imagine them becoming fast friends. The connection gave her hope.

Finally, Mrs. Hamilton rose to leave, reiterating her invitation to the women's auxiliary meeting. Amelia would do her best to fit in even if she had put on a disingenuous face at first. Once the ladies were gone, she was confronted by a silent and empty house. Josiah was supposedly writing his sermon, and Mrs. Drinkwater had gone to the village.

The vicarage did not yet feel like her home. Would it ever? She slipped out the door and weaved her way through the gravestones to the church. It was empty. No foreigner stashed in the vestry and no Josiah working on his sermon. She was not surprised.

She glanced down the pretty lane that led from the church to the village. Meeting more of the village without Josiah by her side to smooth the way was untenable. She cursed his absence, feeling abandoned. Sitting alone in the vicarage was not appealing either. Instead, she strolled toward the copse behind the church.

The undergrowth was thick and brambly and impassable, but Hanson had said he would leave this way with the German. It took a keen eye and a good quarter hour of searching to locate the narrow footpath. She gathered her skirts close to her body to avoid them being snagged and made her way under the arms of the pines and hardwoods.

A deep breath of loamy air settled her nerves. Finally, something that was familiar. Her childhood had been spent exploring the woods and dales around their manor, usually trailing behind her brother Daniel. The rustling of small creatures and the buzzing insects had only piqued her curiosity as a child, never any fear.

She continued on, shedding the stress brought on by the uncertainty of the past weeks. It seemed impossible how thoroughly and swiftly her life had changed. She was a married woman now with responsibilities. How soon before she became a mother? She stopped in the middle of the copse.

Even younger women in much less favorable circumstances than she birthed babes every day, yet Amelia wasn't ready. Was any woman ready? That was an interesting thought. She wished she could ask her mother. A shard of grief grew hot in her heart.

She leaned against a nearby pine, its scent tangy and sharp. A rustling in the underbrush had her squatting down. Was it a little field mouse? She had kept one as a pet for a few weeks when she was ten. She had adored its little whiskers and bright eyes.

She lifted the branch of the low bush nearest to her, a flash of red startling her. It was an unnatural color to be found in the woods. She squinted. It appeared to be cloth. Crouching even lower, she moved closer and reached into the shadows.

She recoiled. Her brain worked to catch up with what she had felt. Skin. Cold skin.

She wasn't sure how long she remained crouched, but her knees were stiff when she stood. Nothing was visible from the higher vantage point. She pushed the branches apart, ignoring the sting of scratches on her hands.

A man stared up at her. Her breathing grew shallow and her heart was pounding so viscously all she could hear was her own blood speeding through her body. It was Heinrich, the German, and he was obviously dead. It wasn't just his blank eyes and the blue cast to his skin that told her. It was the gaping wound across his throat.

She had no idea how long she stood there staring at him. She had tended to her mother in her final days, but her passing had been gradual and peaceful. There was nothing peaceful about the way Heinrich had died. The fingernails on the one hand that was visible were torn and crusted with either dirt or blood.

She let go of the branches, and they snapped back to conceal the German from sight once more. But the image of the dead man was burned into her head and would not soon be erased. Who had killed him? Hanson? Or was that man's body stashed under a bush somewhere too?

A shiver crawled up her neck, and she looked over her shoulder. No one was there. Or at least, no one she could see. The birds still chirped and the leaves overhead rustled. But any peace she had gained had been snatched away by her discovery.

Josiah. He would know what to do.

She abandoned any pretense of ladylike behavior, gathering her skirts to her knees and retracing her steps down the narrow path. Brambles tore at her stockings, but she only picked up her pace. The vicarage came into view through the trees when her skirts caught in a thorn bush, unbalancing her. She hit the ground on her hands and knees, the jolt painful.

A noise like the crack of a branch sounded somewhere behind her. Her fear had become tangible, and she scrambled up, tugging her skirts free with a rending of fabric. She burst out of the copse into the clearing behind the vicarage and kept running until she threw herself inside.

Josiah strode out of the sitting room, his eyes widening when he saw her. His surprise only lasted a moment. His jaw tightened, and he took her elbow to guide her into the sitting room. "What happened?"

Her breath came in quick bursts, partly through exertion and partly through the fear that had weakened her knees. She pointed. "Heinrich."

"What about him?"

"He's dead."

He didn't blink an eye at her pronouncement. "Where?"

"In the copse. Under a bush by the trail. Difficult to see."

Josiah moved to the sideboard, poured amber liquid into a glass, and returned to press it into her hands. "Drink this. Don't move. I'll be back in a moment."

She took the glass in one hand and grabbed his lapel in the other. "What if the murderer is still out there?"

"Then I will deal with him." Danger lurked in his voice. Whatever happened, it was clear Josiah could handle himself. She was relieved but also wondered at the secrets of the man she had married. What horrors had he experienced during the war?

Daniel's letters home had glossed over the worst of it, she was sure. A wellspring of emotion bubbled through the shock and fear of discovering Heinrich. She released his jacket. "Go. We must discover who did this and why."

"We?" His eyebrows lifted.

"*We*. I assured Heinrich he would be safe. I feel responsible."

"Your guilt is misplaced, but we will have to discuss that later." He leaned in to press a hard, bracing kiss on her lips and left.

Her hands throbbed and she looked at them for the first time. The backs were crisscrossed with red scratches, but only one was deep enough to trickle blood. The palms of her hands were red from catching her fall. Her legs and knees were similarly injured. Her dress was dirty and torn and would have to be cleaned and mended. All minor compared to what had happened to Heinrich.

As she washed her hands at the basin in the kitchen, she wondered how long would it take to stop seeing his lifeless eyes and slit throat every time she closed her eyes? She peeked out the kitchen window toward the line of trees, willing Josiah to return to her.

It seemed like an eternity, but the clock hadn't even chimed a quarter hour when Josiah emerged from the woods. His gait was long and fluid, his expression pensive. He was a man comfortable with his physicality and decisive in his movements. Warmth kindled in her chest. It wasn't desire, but appreciation and thankfulness. In spite of the fact a murder had taken place on their doorstep, she felt safe for the first time in months.

She met him at the door. "Did you find him?"

"Right where you said he would be." He looked even more troubled than when he'd left.

"Any sign of Hanson?"

"None."

Their shared suspicions didn't need voice. "What now?"

"Now, I must ride with haste to London. If Sir Gray hasn't already departed for the country, I shall enlist his aid. Otherwise, I'll have to scare up someone from the Home Office to listen to me." He was already making preparations.

"What about Heinrich? Should I inform the magistrate so the body can be retrieved?"

Josiah turned and took her upper arms in a firm grip. "You mustn't tell anyone. Not yet. Not even Mrs. Drinkwater. If Hanson returns—" At her gasp, he shook his head. "—Which he has no reason to do—I want him to think his subterfuge has not yet been discovered."

"How long will you be gone?"

"I'll return as soon as possible."

She wanted to hug him to her and not let go. What was stopping her? He was her husband, after all. She wrapped her arms around him and rested her forehead against his neck. Only when he let out a long breath and relaxed into her embrace did she realize how tense he was. "Are you worried?"

"About myself? No."

"About me?"

"I vowed to protect you. I fear I am botching it already." He rubbed his jaw against her temple. The sweetly affectionate gesture made her tighten her hold.

"Was it only yesterday I found you again?" she asked aloud, but the question wasn't directed at him but at fate itself. Now that it had happened, it felt inevitable. The wide-eyed infatuation of her youth was morphing into something deeper and richer. She wasn't ready to put a name to it lest it crumble under the weight.

"If I am to return to you by this evening, I must leave."

Their goodbye was a kiss of such intensity her world felt unbalanced afterward. She saw him off from the narrow lane and only returned to the vicarage when he was out of sight. A shiver coursed through her that had nothing to do with the misty rain beginning to fall.

She trudged up the stairs to their chambers to change gowns. With her mind on Josiah's progress, she shook out her torn, dirty gown. A piece of parchment fell at her feet, the crumbling wax seal visible.

She muttered a curse and pick the missive up with trembling fingers. How could she have forgotten what Heinrich had entrusted to her? To be fair, much had happened since that moment, but still. Foreboding flooded her. Was this why Heinrich was killed?

She tapped the letter to her palm, debating what to do. If only she had remembered the letter before Josiah had left. But, she hadn't. Waffling for a moment, she made her decision, breaking what was left of the seal and moving to the window to catch the meager light.

As always, she did much better reading German and was able to piece together the gist of the letter. There was no indication who the letter was from or to, but it detailed the assassination Heinrich had mentioned and an uprising against the German Confederation. How many lives was this information worth? At least one, it would seem.

She tucked the letter between the pages of one of Austen's novels she had not yet found a place for and went downstairs to wait. Her advantage was that no one knew she had the letter. The killer, presumably Hanson, only knew that Heinrich was not in possession of it, if he even knew it existed. And if he did, Heinrich could have disposed of it anywhere and at any time since leaving the Continent. She took a deep breath and calmed her nerves.

Mrs. Drinkwater had returned to put together an evening meal, and Amelia was glad to not be alone in the house. When she entered the kitchen, Mrs. Drinkwater looked up from where she was cutting potatoes and dropping them in a pot. "Where is Mr. Barrymore?"

"He had urgent business in London, but will return tonight."

"Is anything amiss?" Mrs. Drinkwater's gaze was sharp.

"Nothing that I'm aware of." Amelia met the older woman's gaze and didn't allow herself to flinch or falter. Mrs. Drinkwater would be safer not knowing a body had been hidden in the copse.

The stew finished simmering and still Josiah had not returned. Amelia couldn't keep herself from pacing the sitting room and checking out the window more times than was good for her sanity.

"I brought you a tray since the master isn't home yet. I'll leave the pot simmering for him. He'll need warming if he rides back in this weather." Mrs. Drinkwater set down a tray with a bowl of steaming stew and a hearty hunk of bread. "I'll be off to my own hearth unless you'd like me to stay."

"I know he appreciates all you do. We both do." Amelia did want her to stay. Badly. Yet she forced a smile. "I'll be fine. Thank you."

Amelia was alone. She tried to eat, but each spoonful settled in her stomach like stones. The sound of a horse approaching had her running out the front, but even in the gloaming she could tell it wasn't Josiah approaching. The horse had four white socks unlike Josiah's bay horse.

Amelia took slow steps backward toward the door. It was useless, of course. She had already exposed herself. Hanson dismounted and left his horse to snuffle at the grass at the edge of the graveyard.

Amelia had a decision to make. She could lock herself inside the vicarage thus letting Hanson know she knew he was a murderer and traitor. Or she could welcome Hanson in and attempt to fool him until Josiah returned.

Hanson was a big man who could easily break inside the vicarage and overpower her. She only had one choice.

Forcing an end to her retreat, she pasted a smile on her face. "Mr. Hanson? Was my husband expecting you?"

"Maybe." Hanson pushed his way by her to stomp through the downstairs rooms, coming to a stop in the entry to face her. "Where is he?"

"He is out tending to one of his parishioners."

"His horse is gone."

"At a farmhouse down the road. Not in town." Amelia forced her expression to remain as neutral as possible even as she could do nothing about her quickened, nervous breathing. "He'll be home soon. If you would like to wait at the inn, I can—"

"I'll wait here." Hanson shook out his greatcoat before moving into the sitting room and helping himself to a large glass of liquor on the sideboard.

Amelia remained in the doorway. Could she possibly slip out? She could start down the road to London to warn Josiah. She had just slid her foot backward when Hanson spun around to glare at her.

"Come in and sit." He pointed to one of the armchairs.

"I need to—"

"You need to sit and answer my questions. Did the German leave anything here?"

An image of the letter tucked into the book upstairs sprang to mind, but she made a show of pretending to think about his question before shaking her head. "He came with the clothes on his back and left the same way. He was only here a few hours. Does he think he forgot something?"

Hanson grunted and tossed back another swallow of liquor, grimacing slightly. "No, but I do. Did he stay upstairs?"

"Yes. In the room with the cot."

Hanson heaved himself out of the chair and trudged upstairs, his boots clomping through the rooms. Amelia's fingers twisted together on her lap. He would find nothing in the room the German had occupied, and there was no reason for him to rifle through her books.

He returned with an annoyed look on his face. Relieved, she took a deep breath and cast her gaze down. The scratches stood out against the white skin of her hands, and she tucked them under her legs, hoping Hanson had not noticed.

"I'm hungry," he announced.

"Mrs. Drinkwater left stew on to simmer."

"Get me a bowl." Hanson swung his head around to glare at her. "A strong cup of coffee wouldn't go amiss either."

Amelia wanted to tell him to go straight to hell, but the man before her was a murderer, and she doubted poor Heinrich was the first victim. Being a lady would not save her. She rose and retreated to the kitchen. Hanson followed her and watched her work which only frayed her nerves more.

She burned her already damaged hands twice when trying to heat water for his coffee. The stew was easy enough to dole out. He sat heavily in a kitchen chair and ate with a sloppy enthusiasm that turned her stomach. She took his empty bowl in order to wash it.

He grabbed her wrist. "What is this?"

"I burned my hand." The angry welt stood in contrast to the narrow scratches. She tried to tug her hand free, but his hold only tightened.

He expelled a long breath, his nostrils flaring. "You discovered my handiwork, didn't you?"

"What? No!" The trilling squeakiness of her voice was too loud. She cleared her throat and tried again. "I have no idea what you're talking about, Mr. Hanson."

He tossed her hand away and pushed to his feet, leaning over the table on his fists to glare at her. "I should have known. You treated me like I was no better than muck on the bottom of your shoe earlier, and now you call me Mister? You found Heinrich. I should have dragged him deeper into the woods."

There was no use lying. "You killed him."

"Yes." The admission was cold and held no guilt or remorse. "Where is the letter?"

She had to lie about it and make it as convincing as possible or she would end up under a bush with her throat slit, too. "I am aware of no letter."

"Did he give it to Barrymore? Has he taken it to London?" Anger tinged with desperation rose in Hanson's voice.

"I told you, Josiah is tending to an ill parishioner." She forced her gaze to stay steady on his.

"You may be telling the truth, or you may be lying. It's easy enough to find out." He took a sweeping glance around the kitchen. His smile sent a quiver straight to Amelia's knees. He picked up a knife. "Will your new husband still want you if your face is cut up like ribbons?"

She grabbed the edge of the table, fear making it difficult to think logically. A man who would slit another's throat and toss them to nature to feast on would cut her without a second thought. Should she hand over the letter?

Mrs. Drinkwater's admonishment to Josiah on her arrival flitted through her head. Amelia did not want to be a weakness. The letter was important. Could she hold out somehow until Josiah returned? Would a prayer do any good?

A clatter came up the lane to the vicarage, and Amelia looked heavenward in thanks. If it was Josiah, he wasn't alone. She could hear the call of more than one man and laughter. Amelia and Hanson were frozen in place.

"Sister! Dear, Sister! Where are you?" A sing-song voice slurred the words out.

Any other time she would curse her brother's arrival on her doorstep. This time she might just throw her arms around him in a hug. A pounding sounded on the front door.

"It's my brother. He will not be put off."

Hanson cursed and brandished the knife at her. "Get rid of him."

Hanson was behind her when she cracked open the front door. If James had been alone, she might have followed Hanson's orders. As much of a degenerate as James had turned into, he was still her brother. Hanson would kill him.

But James was not alone. Four equally degenerate companions had accompanied him. One drove an open-topped racing phaeton, and the others were on horseback. All of them were skunked, but they were gentlemen born. They would have learned to box and use a sword at the very least.

When she opened the door, James pushed his way inside. "Sister. You are coming with me. Don't throw your life away on this vicar." James gestured toward Hanson who was behind her. "The marriage can be annulled. Spencer here has agreed to wed you. He's a decent bloke."

The man behind James tipped his rakishly set hat and grinned at her. He looked like a bounder with nothing but pudding between his ears.

"I've been awaiting your arrival, brother. We should depart forthwith," Amelia said. "Let me retrieve my bonnet and cloak."

"No!" Hanson yelled, but it made little impact over the eruption of chatter from the young gentlemen congratulating themselves on a well-executed abduction.

Amelia grabbed her bonnet and cloak from the hook and followed her brother out of the door. At least the misty rain had stopped. Hanson trailed her, grabbing her arm before Spencer could hand her up into the high phaeton.

"You can't leave," Hanson said.

Amelia shrugged. "I must. This is my brother. He is my only kin, and he demands my marriage be annulled."

"That's ridiculous." Hanson wasn't stomping his feet, but he was looking distinctly unsettled.

It really was ridiculous, but she could play her part in the farce so long as she escaped Hanson. She would figure out how to escape James later when her life wasn't hanging in the balance.

"Perhaps you should call on Mr. Barrymore tomorrow," Amelia said to Hanson as she took Spencer's hand and hauled herself onto the narrow seat.

"But—"

The clack of the phaeton's wheels over the rocks drowned out whatever protest Hanson was about to make. It would have been satisfying to watch Hanson's frustration at her abrupt departure if she hadn't gained several new problems. One was how to escape from her rescuers. Second was how to get a warning to Josiah before he walked into a trap upon his return.

Her brother trotted his fine horse next to her. He wobbled in the saddle, his face a mask of satisfaction. It would be a miracle if he didn't fall and break his neck before they reached London.

"Thought we were going to have to tie you up and throw you in,"

James said.

"How absolutely horrid of you." Her truthful pronouncement fell on dumb ears.

"Glad I didn't have to use this," Spencer added jovially. He set a dueling pistol on the carriage seat between them.

Lanterns hung from hooks at the front of the phaeton casting a wavering light over his face and onto the road ahead. The misty rain had given way to a rising fog, forcing them to travel at a slow pace. Could she leap out of the phaeton without causing herself harm? Unfortunately, it was set stylishly high and impractical.

As she was considering other possibilities, her opportunity presented itself. One of the men on horseback decided he needed to make water which prompted all of them to dismount to stand along the side of the lane.

Spencer squirmed on the seat. Amelia turned to him with a sweet smile. "I'd be happy to hold the reins if you need to join your friends."

"Thank you. I'd be most grateful." Spencer clambered down.

Amelia wasted no time. With the pistol in hand, she lowered herself to the ground, and then for good measure, slapped the rump of the horse. The carriage jerked forward. Laughter turned into panicked calls and her brother and his friends fumbled with their breeches as they ran after the phaeton.

Amelia melted back into the verge along the side of the lane. They hadn't traveled far. Surely, she could find her way back to the vicarage. If she waited long enough, she could probably walk back the way she came.

She underestimated how determined her brother was to haul her back to London for an annulment. He and his friends walked up and down the lane for what seemed an age, calling her name, and peering into the fog. None were brave enough to actually venture into the shadows. She waited until they had moved to the other side before creeping farther into the brush, trying her best not to rustle the branches.

She straightened and looked around. In the distance, a deeper darkness lurked. Was that the copse behind the vicarage? She tightened her hold on the pistol. She was about to find out.

CHAPTER TEN

Josiah pushed his mount harder than was wise in the fog, but urgency beat at him like a whip. Sir Gray was on his heels. It had been luck that Sir Gray was still in London. A broken carriage wheel had held off his travel for a day. Josiah could only hope his luck held.

The two men were silent. The implications of the German's death were already reverberating through Sir Gray's network of spies. Trust was a commodity beyond price, and Josiah knew at that moment Sir Gray felt poor.

He veered left at the fork in the road. Home was only a few moments away now, but he was more anxious than ever. He had to slow when he came upon a phaeton and several riders dismounted and arguing in the middle of the lane.

"Good evening, sirs!" Josiah called out and came to a stop.

Sir Gray stayed behind him, and a glance showed the man had pulled his hat lower so as not to be recognized. While Josiah did not know any of the men, they appeared to be part of polite society in their Bond Street tailored suits and Hoby boots.

The men cast nervous glances at one another and the hairs on the back of Josiah's neck quivered. "Can I be of service?" he asked.

"No, indeed. We were merely making water. Let's be on our way, lads." The leader of the group mounted, and the others followed. While it was obvious they were all foxed, something had sobered them to the point of silence.

Once they were on their way, Sir Gray guided his horse next to Josiah. "Did you recognize the fellow who spoke?"

"No. Should I have?"

"It was James Fielding."

Josiah started and swung around in the saddle to watch the retreating light of the lanterns. Panic coursed through him. "What? He must have come for Amelia."

"But he obviously didn't find her. There was nowhere to hide her in that phaeton."

Far from offering comfort, Sir Gray's words only made Josiah's worry rise. He had promised to keep Amelia safe, and he was failing spectacularly on all fronts. Tapping his horse's flanks with his heels, he picked up the pace. Every dip of the road was familiar to him. At the turn into the lane, he dismounted. Sir Gray followed his lead, although he raised a brow in Josiah's direction.

"It never hurts to be cautious," Josiah whispered.

After leaving their mounts tied at the edge of the lane, the two men stalked closer to the vicarage. Light seeped around the curtains at the sitting room window. Was Amelia waiting for him in front of a cozy fire? The light should have reassured him, but it didn't.

Josiah pushed the door open. It was silent. He made sure it was well-oiled. Careful, soft steps brought him to the sitting room door, Sir Gray on his heels. The room was empty, but a tumbler with a swallow of liquor left in it sat on the table.

Sir Gray was shoved into Josiah, both of them stumbling into the room. Hanson stood in the doorway brandishing a wickedly sharp-looking hunting knife in one hand and a knife from the vicarage's kitchen in the other.

"Where is it?" Hanson asked gruffly.

"Where is Amelia?" Josiah asked.

"She's gone." The cold finality of Hanson's blunt statement made Josiah's head swimmy. Had Hanson killed her? Before the thought could take hold, Hanson added, "Your wife took off with her brother to seek an annulment, my friend." A mean little smile turned Hanson's lips.

"You are no friend of mine, you blackguard." Josiah's mind raced over what he knew as he and Sir Gray shifted subtly into positions of readiness, wary eyes on Hanson and his knives. If Hanson was to be believed, Amelia had left with James, but she was clearly no longer with her brother. What if the men had done something nefarious and Amelia was lying on the side of the lane injured, or worse? His panic rose, but he recognized it and quickly clamped down on his emotions like he'd learned to do during the war. A bit of logic seeped through.

James did not want Amelia dead. Her death would ruin any chance he had to obtain her inheritance. Plus, Amelia was not meek or cowardly. He would bet everything he owned down to his stockings that she had slipped out of James's clutches and was seeking help in the village.

Despite his vocation, he wasn't a praying man outside of Sunday services. But now he found himself lobbing a desperate plea to God to keep Amelia clear of the messy business about to take place in the sitting room. He hoped they didn't leave too big a mess or Mrs. Drinkwater would ring a peal over his head tomorrow.

Josiah exchanged a telling glance with Sir Gray. In spite of the fact he was knighted, married to the sister of an earl, and circulated in polite society, Sir Gray Masterson was willing and more than able to get his hands dirty. It was the two of them against Hanson, and even with Hanson wielding two knives, Josiah would take those odds.

"Was your wife disappointed in your manly abilities, son?" Hanson was using a well-worn technique to prod Josiah into a rash attack.

"I'm well rid of her," Josiah said with a nonchalant shrug.

Hanson harrumphed, his expression hardening. "Where's the letter?"

"What letter?" Sir Gray interjected.

"The letter the German left."

"There was no letter, Hanson." Josiah exchanged another glance with Sir Gray. They would need to coordinate their advance on Hanson so neither were at the mercy of his weapons.

Hanson let out a long breath. "I was assured there was a letter. I need it."

"Why?" Sir Gray slid his foot closer to Hanson, and Josiah followed his lead.

"Someone is willing to pay good coin for it. My life is done for, ain't it?" He directed the question toward Sir Gray.

"That's generally what happens to traitors, Hanson," Sir Gray said solemnly.

"I'm no traitor. This information has nothing to do with England. It's the Germans who will pay, and I need the money to sail to America. Everything has gone to shit."

Josiah almost felt sorry for him. Almost. Hanson's greed had been his undoing. It was the undoing of many a man, Amelia's brother, James, included. Apparently, the lesson must be learned over and over again. Perhaps that would be the content of his Sunday sermon.

"There is no letter," Josiah repeated. "There will be no coin for you."

"And no escape," added Sir Gray.

"We'll see about that. You—" Hanson gestured to Josiah with the long blade. "Tie him up." He pointed the kitchen knife at Sir Gray.

Before he and Sir Gray could rush Hanson, the unmistakable click of a pistol being cocked reverberated, and a cool voice said, "Drop the weapons, sirrah."

Hanson didn't have a chance to turn before the muzzle of the pistol was pressed against the back of his head.

"Drop the knives and sit down," Amelia repeated.

Amelia looked like she'd been through hell and back. Her hair fell around her shoulders in wet tangles. Twigs and leaves stuck out at various angles. The hem of her dress was ripped, streaked with brown, and dripping muddy water on the floor. An angry red scratch followed the color across her cheekbone.

"You'll not kill me. You're a lady." Hanson sneered, but he had frozen in place.

"I'm not feeling much like a lady right now. More like a Valkyrie ready to escort you to hell." The cold anger in her voice was frankly terrifying. "Although, perhaps, I should reserve the bullet for my husband who is well rid of me."

Hanson's eyes were wide and unblinking when he looked toward Josiah. The knives clattered to the floor, and Hanson sat in the armchair, looking suddenly meek.

Josiah half-expected Amelia to train the pistol on him, but she only lowered her hand to point the muzzle at the floor, uncocking it. The tension in the room dissipated. While Sir Gray dealt with Hanson, Josiah took three ground-swallowing steps to Amelia. He gripped the barrel of the gun and tugged, but she did not release it.

"You know I didn't mean that. I was trying to convince Hanson."

"Convince him of what?"

"Convince him I do not care for you. It would have been more dangerous for him to know the truth."

"And what is the truth?" The intensity of her gaze made it clear she would not accept evasions or half-truths.

"I find myself struggling with how strong my feelings are for you, Amelia. It is shocking. Disconcerting. Unbelievable even."

"What is so unbelievable?"

"How important you've become to me in such a short amount of time. Or maybe, you were always important to me."

"Because I am Daniel's sister?" She tilted her head slightly, her eyes warming to the blue of a summer sky he wanted to bask in.

"Because you are brave and beautiful and . . . *mine*. Mine forever. There is no escaping me."

"As if I want to. I only left with James because the alternative was getting sliced and diced by Hanson for information on the letter."

She finally loosened her grip on the gun, and he set it aside to push the hair off her face. "There is no letter."

"Yes. There is."

Josiah thought Sir Gray otherwise occupied tying Hanson up with the decorative rope from the curtains, which Mrs. Drinkwater would be livid about in the morning, but he turned to them and asked, "You have the letter, Mrs. Barrymore?"

"I do. Upstairs tucked into my favorite Austen novel."

Hanson spat out a string of curses and rocked in his bonds. He was ignored.

"Will you retrieve it for me?" Sir Gray asked.

Amelia looked to Josiah, and he nodded. She fetched the letter and handed it to Sir Gray.

"You read it?" he asked, tapping the broken seal.

"I did. I had forgotten Heinrich had given me the letter after I discovered him in the vestry." She sent Josiah an apologetic look. "I don't think he entirely trusted you. I had tucked it into my dress, but so much happened in such a short amount of time, it slipped my mind until I went to change my dress after discovering his body. You had already left for London."

"Can I count on your discretion, Mrs. Barrymore?" Sir Gray asked.

"Of course. You will let us give Heinrich a proper burial, won't you?"

"If that's what you wish," Sir Gray said. "You'll see to it, Barrymore?"

"I have just the place," Josiah said dryly, glancing toward the graveyard.

"One less problem for me to clean up." Sir Gray hauled Hanson to his feet. "I'll need to borrow your carriage, Barrymore, to get this miscreant to London."

"Of course. I can ride in to retrieve it from your town house mews in a day or two." Josiah turned to Amelia. "You must be cold and exhausted. Why don't you go upstairs and get warm while I see Sir Gray off?"

"I am a bit worse for wear." She stopped in the hallway to ask in a low voice, "What will happen to him?"

Josiah glanced at Hanson. If she asked the question earlier that day, he might be tempted to gloss over what would come next, but she had more than proven herself brave enough for the whole truth. "He will die."

"After a trial? Will there be a public hanging outside of Newgate?"

"No. His betrayal will not be made public. He knows too much. Someone from the Home Office will deal with him after they extract any useful information."

She merely nodded, and he watched her disappear toward the kitchen, presumably to heat water. Even after everything—or maybe because of everything—his imagination imprinted an image of a very naked Amelia sponging herself clean.

"Come on, Barrymore," Sir Gray said impatiently while attempting to manhandle a fighting Hanson out the door.

It took a half-hour to subdue Hanson. A knock on the back of the head helped matters. After his legs had been bound and a gag tied to keep him as quiet as possible, Sir Gray and Josiah heaved him under the carriage seat.

Josiah looked up at Sir Gray who was setting the reins. "You'll deal with him appropriately? I don't want Amelia put at risk."

"Don't worry, he won't be bothering you or your wife again." Sir Gray clicked his tongue and slapped the reins. It would be a miserable ride back to London, and Josiah was heartily grateful Sir Gray hadn't asked for his help. His priorities had shifted, and Josiah wasn't sure what to make of it yet, but it felt . . . good. Right.

Amelia was downstairs in the sitting room. Her face was scrubbed clean and her hair combed and loose around her shoulders. She was wearing his dressing gown, the sleeves rolled up and the hem dragging along the floor as she paced. Her white nightrail peeked out on each turn.

"Feeling better?" He held out his arms.

She let out a gusty sigh upon seeing him and walked straight into his embrace. "Much. It took me forever to bumble through the woods to the back of the vicarage. It was so dark and the path difficult to find. That's two dresses I've ruined in as many days."

"I'll introduce you to the local seamstress tomorrow." He stroked her hair, marveling at its silky, springy texture. "By the way, I came across your brother and his friends. They were still looking for you, but seemed to give it up when I asked a few questions."

"He might be mostly incompetent, but I worry he'll try again."

"While I will certainly have strong words with him as soon as possible—my calling be damned—I have full confidence in your ability to handle him. Look at what you reduced Hanson to, and he's a treasonous murderer."

"I was terrified for you and then furious at you."

"You do believe me when I say I didn't mean a word of it?" He cupped her face and tilted it up.

Her smile was answer enough, and he kissed her gently—at first. It didn't take long for their kiss to deepen and grow in intensity. He fumbled with the ties of his dressing gown and slipped it off her shoulders to puddle on the floor at their feet.

She turned her head to the side, her breaths coming rapidly. "What are you doing?"

Trailing his lips down her neck, he said, "Fucking my wife if she's agreeable."

Her head fell back to offer greater access. "She is more than agreeable."

After an evening filled with danger and worries, the tension inside him craved the most primitive of releases. Based on Amelia's clutching hands as she pushed his shirt over his head, she was feeling a similar urge.

They fumbled with the placard of his trousers together, their laughter doing little to dampen the desperation building between them. While plundering her mouth, he pushed her against the nearest wall.

She gasped against his mouth. "Are we . . . ?"

He smiled, fisted the skirt of her nightrail, and pulled it to her waist in answer. Sliding his hands under her bare buttocks, he lifted her. Her legs rose and clamped his hips. His cock was hard and straining against her core. His need to be inside her made him clumsy, but finally he sank into her wet heat deeper than he thought possible.

His knees trembled at the pleasure already coursing through him. He wouldn't last long, and his only hope was that she was battling the same insistent desire after the harrowing night. He took a sharp thrust and then another.

She reached out and grabbed the mantle to the right, knocking off a brass candleholder, the candles extinguishing on their fall. It clattered to the floor but only spurred him on faster and harder.

He cupped her buttocks, reveling in the softness of her body cradling him. Her nightrail fell off one shoulder, the curve of her breast a sight for his gaze to feast on. Her hair bounced with every thrust, and her nails dug into his neck where she was holding on to him.

She was magnificent.

He had never considered himself a lucky man, but with his mind cleared of everything except the feel of her body and scent of her arousal, he could see the path the fates had guided him down to arrive at this moment. He'd been lucky to find a friend in Daniel, lucky again to survive the war, and luckiest of all to marry Amelia. It had all been connected.

She bit her lip and let out a moan as her inner walls convulsed around his cock. He let himself fall into the abyss of pleasure alongside her, bucking his hips into hers with a ferocity he couldn't help. Finally, they stilled, except for their panting breaths. He leaned into her, his knees weak, his forehead resting against the wall at her temple.

"That was amazing." She sounded like a sleepy kitten having finished a bowl of cream.

"Agreed." He lowered her legs to the floor, and she stumbled against him. "I didn't hurt you, did I?"

"Did I sound hurt?"

He chuckled. "You sounded well pleased."

They collapsed across the settee, their limbs intertwined.

"No, I was *very* well pleased."

The candles that they hadn't knocked over had burned low when he found enough energy to move. While he could have remained on the settee with her all night, Mrs. Drinkwater would have been scandalized to walk in on them in such a state of dishabille in the morning. She would already be put out with the loss of the curtain ties and all the splattered wax.

Before tucking her into bed, he disposed of her nightrail and his trousers and cuddled her in his arms, skin-to-skin, with no secrets left between them.

EPILOGUE

Three months later

MUCH TO HER surprise, Sundays were Amelia's favorite day of the week. She counted many of the parishioners as friends, especially Miss Grace Hamilton. Having grown up with two brothers, she had always wished for a sister, and in Grace she had found one.

She had taken to helping Josiah with his sermons, focusing less on sin and fire and brimstone, and more on the daily struggles of life she observed all around them like grief and pride and envy.

Her brother, James, had sold their family home and left England. She suspected she would never hear from him again. Amelia mourned his loss as much as Daniel's. Her family was Josiah and Mrs. Drinkwater and Grace and all the other inhabitants of Upper Wexham now.

Josiah still worked for the Home Office. Of course, it made her nervous when he set off on one of Sir Gray's tasks, but none had proved as dangerous as Heinrich, whose plot she tended in the far corner of the graveyard. She often wondered about his family and whether they knew he was dead and if they grieved.

But now it was late Sunday afternoon and the very favorite part of her favorite day. Mrs. Drinkwater had the afternoon off and Josiah's ministerial tasks were finished. She and her husband had the vicarage to themselves. Most of the time they retreated to the big comfortable bed in their chambers. But sometimes, they didn't make it past the settee or the armchair or, once, the dining table.

A soft rain fell outside, feeding the explosion of flowers around the churchyard. Tomorrow she would tend to them, but currently she was tending to her husband. They were cocooned under the covers, both breathing hard from their exertions. The marriage bed had proved to be pleasurable and downright fun.

It hadn't taken long to put voice to their growing feelings for one another. Weeks had passed since Josiah's whispered confession of love one night. She had kissed him senseless and told him the same. It was difficult to imagine her life without him.

She owed Mrs. Dove-Lyon a debt she could never repay. If the Widow of Whitehall hadn't interfered and forced Amelia into marriage, where would she have ended up? As an upstairs girl at the Lyon's Den?

She held onto Josiah even tighter at the thought of treading down that path.

A rapping sounded on the front door of the vicarage and Josiah raised his head off the pillow. "Who the devil could that be in this weather?"

"Perhaps someone has taken ill." Amelia was already swinging her legs off the bed. She dropped a chemise over her head and pulled on Josiah's dressing gown. "Or it could be Sir Gray. You'd better go answer it."

"Sir Gray would never do anything so obvious as knock on the front door. The man enjoys the subterfuge a little too much." Josiah grumbled and dressed quickly.

The knock came again, more forcefully this time. Josiah clomped down the stairs. Amelia waited at the top in order to listen but remain unseen.

Josiah opened the door. Amelia could only see the hem of a dark gray gown and scuffed boots on the other side.

"Can I help you, girl?" Josiah's voice had softened considerably.

A girl? How old? A very old worn carpetbag was shifted to hang in front of the girl whose hands were bare.

"I'm B-Bess, sir."

"Hello, Bess. I'm Josiah Barrymore, the vicar."

"I was sent." Her voice was small and tremulous and sounded close to tears. Even though Josiah was doing his best to be gentle in his handling of the girl, it was obvious she was scared.

"By whom?"

The girl struggled to speak, and Amelia decided she should insert herself. She glided down the stairs, taking in the entirety of the waif on their doorstep. She was young and as skinny as a reed. Mousy brown hair stuck out of a simple bonnet that had been patched and was frayed around the edges. Her dress was in similar shape, and the carpet bag she carried had a broken handle and looked mostly empty.

Her face was pale, and her cheekbones sharp. Her features were even and pretty, her heavily fringed amber eyes her best and most distinctive feature. But there were deep shadows underneath as if she hadn't had a decent night's sleep or enough to eat for too long. She shivered, either from the rain or nerves.

Amelia pushed Josiah aside, put an arm around the girl, and swept her into the sitting room. Embers from an earlier fire to chase the cool morning air away still glowed, and Amelia moved one of the arm-chairs closer, urging the girl to sit.

She took the bag out of the girl's cold, stiff fingers and handed it to Josiah.

"Wait. That's mine." The girl tried to rise, but Amelia sank to her haunches by the chair and patted her leg to settle her back down.

"Your bag is safe here, as are you. I'm Mrs. Barrymore. It's a nasty day for traveling. Can you tell us how you found yourself on our doorstep this afternoon?"

"It was Mrs. Dove-Lyon that sent me." Bess's accent was broad and brought to mind rolling hills and Yorkshire sheep.

"She sent you?"

"Aye. Said you'd take me in as a favor to her. Give me a better life than working upstairs at the Lyon's Den."

"How old are you, Bess?" Amelia asked.

"Eleven."

Amelia exchanged a telling look with Josiah. It was heartbreaking to think of an eleven-year-old girl forced to sell herself to survive. She couldn't consider the fact there were men who would pay for the privilege.

"Where is your family, Bess?" Josiah asked.

"North. There are too many of us to feed. Once we turn ten, Ma sets us loose. Two of me brothers already left to London. Tried to find them, but—" She shook her head. "No idea a place could have so many people in it."

"London can be overwhelming, can't it? Upper Wexham is a lovely size. You'll like it here," Amelia said.

Bess's shoulders straightened from their hunch slightly. "I can stay?"

"Of course. There is a small room upstairs you can use."

"I'm a hard worker, I am." Bess scooted to the edge of the chair.

"I'm sure you are. What sort of work would you like to do?" Amelia asked.

"I like to cook. Ma almost kept me on 'cause I knew me way 'round a kitchen. Always wanted to work in the kitchen of a fine house."

Amelia nodded and rose. "Until we can see you in a more advantageous situation, you can apprentice with Mrs. Drinkwater, our cook and housekeeper. But for now, I'll heat you some water and some stew. Let's get you into some dry clothes and into bed. You must be exhausted."

Amelia brushed off Bess's insistence she shouldn't be waited on and got her settled in the small room with the cot. Once Bess had warm water and hot stew, Amelia and Josiah retreated to the kitchen to drink cups of tea.

Josiah shook his head. "Mrs. Dove-Lyon said I would owe her a favor. I suppose it's come due."

"A favor for what service?" Amelia looked at him over the rim of her cup as she took a sip. He really was the most handsome man.

"For the special license making our hasty marriage a reality. I would never have been able to procure one myself."

"It's funny, I was thinking earlier how much I owe Mrs. Dove-Lyon for contacting you and matching us. If she hadn't, I would be as lost as Bess. We can help her, can't we?"

Josiah smiled and reached across the kitchen table to take her hand. "It happens to be our duty to help the less fortunate."

She got up and sat in his lap, giving him a kiss. "You might turn out to be a better vicar than a spy."

"I'm a better everything with you in my life," He brushed her tousled hair over her shoulder.

"Our Sunday afternoons will look a bit different with a young, impressionable girl in the house."

Josiah's lips pursed. "On the other hand, I'm feeling less magnanimous by the second."

Amelia merely laughed and kissed his grumpiness away. She had no doubt they would find time to love one another through all of life's unexpected curves.

Printed in Great Britain
by Amazon

21850093R00066